Happy

New pbk. ed.

BY JERRY WEST

Illustrated by Helen S. Hamilton

THE SVENSON GROUP, INC.
on behalf of The Hollister Family Properties Trust

Text and Illustrations Copyright © 2010
The Svenson Group, Inc.
on behalf of The Hollister Family Properties Trust

ISBN: 1-4528-6506-X
ISBN-13: 9781452865065

Dedication

This new paperback edition of *The Happy Hollisters* is being released in honor of my grandfather, Andrew Edward Svenson. He began the 33-volume series in 1953 using the pseudonym Jerry West. This year we celebrate the 100th anniversary of his birth, and I know he would think it was "swell" that his books still enjoy a loyal following of beginning readers and devoted collectors.

"I guess they just like you, Dad," Pete added.
The boy admired his father greatly,
and had often told Pam that he wanted to
be just like him when he grew up.

I am grateful to the "real" Happy Hollisters for
inspiring my grandfather to write these books,
and for their support of this labor of love:

Andrew E. Svenson, Jr. – "Pete"
Laura Svenson Schnell – "Pam"
Eric R. Svenson, Sr. – "Ricky"
Jane Svenson Kossmann – "Holly"
Eileen Svenson de Zayas and Ingrid Svenson Herdman – "Sue"
And to the "original Mrs. Hollister,"
my grandmother Marian S. Svenson

Andrew E. Svenson, III
The Svenson Group, Inc.
on behalf of The Hollister Family Properties Trust

"It was such fun today," Sue said.
"Can't we do the same thing tomorrow?"
"Swell," Ricky replied. "I'll help you find another adventure!"

Contents

CHAPTER 1

Moving Day

HOLLY HOLLISTER sat on the front steps of her house, looking down the street. The harder she looked, the faster she twirled one of her pigtails.

"Will the moving vans ever come?" she thought impatiently.

This was a big day for the Hollister family. They were moving to another town and a new home.

Suddenly, from around the side of the house raced a young boy. He had reddish hair, and freckles clear to the tip of his turned-up nose.

"Haven't they come yet, Holly?"

"No, Ricky, but I hope they'll get here soon."

"So do I. I want a ride in the moving van!"

Ricky was tall for a seven year old. His long legs seemed to carry him in all directions at once. His blue eyes always sparkled, and he wore a big friendly grin. Holly looked much like her brother except that she had dark hair and brown eyes. When she giggled, her eyes almost closed.

Together the children skipped out to the sidewalk.

"You look one way," Holly said, "and I'll look the other."

Suddenly Ricky let out a whoop. "I see them!" he shouted.

A big moving van and a little one were stopping far down the street. A man hopped off the larger one and walked over to look at a house number. He stopped when he saw the children racing toward him.

"Are you looking for the Happy Hollisters?" Holly burst out.

"We're looking for the Hollister home," replied the man with a smile. "Are you happy about moving?"

"I guess we are," Holly answered.

"Everybody around here calls us the Happy Hollisters," Ricky explained. "Our house is down there," he added, pointing.

"Our house is down there."

"Good. We'll follow you," said the man as he swung up to the seat of the big van.

"We can do it better if we ride with you," Ricky suggested hopefully.

The mover looked at his helper and winked. Then he turned to Ricky and Holly.

"Sure. Hop up here!"

"Thank you, Mr. Moving Man!" Holly said politely.

"Just call me George," he laughed.

Ricky helped Holly up the big step to the front seat, and jumped up himself. The motor rumbled, and the van started down the street, with the smaller one trailing behind. Soon they were in front of the Hollister home.

"May I blow your horn?" Ricky asked.

When George said he might, the little boy honked twice. As he did, another boy and a girl ran out of the front door. The boy was a husky lad of twelve, with sparkling blue eyes and a blond crew hair cut. The girl had fluffy golden hair and brown eyes. She was ten years old and very lively.

"More Happy Hollisters?" George asked.

Ricky nodded. "Our brother and sister, Pete and Pam."

"We have a little sister, too," Holly told him. "Her name is Sue. She's four and always getting into trouble."

"Five Happy Hollisters," grinned George.

"Seven," Holly corrected him. "Our mother and father are happy too."

Pete helped Pam carry out her little maple desk.

By this time the two vans had backed up to the curb, and the men opened the big doors at the rear.

"I want to help you," Ricky said.

"That's a good idea," George replied. "Suppose you children carry your toys to the sidewalk. I see they're on the porch. We'll put them in the second van with the other small stuff."

While the men carried out the heavy pieces of furniture, covering them carefully with blankets to keep them from being scratched, the children toted their toys and games to the small van. Pam and Pete wheeled out their bicycles. Ricky rode Sue's tricycle to the street and lifted it in.

Pete helped Pam carry out her lovely little maple desk. She was very proud of it, and also a set of dolls from various countries. They were packed in cotton and tissue so they could not break. Pam had been collecting the dolls since she was five years old.

"I'll carry your toy piano, Holly," Ricky offered, "just the way the men do."

He had been watching the movers carry out heavy dressers on their backs, holding them on with big straps.

Borrowing one of the long straps, Ricky hurried to the porch and fastened the toy piano onto his back. As he started down the porch steps, his load shifted and teetered. Just in time Pete grabbed it.

But Ricky was not out of trouble yet. The next instant, he tripped on one end of the strap and lost his balance.

Crash!

Ricky and the toy piano hit the ground with a loud jangling noise.

"Oh, Ricky!" Holly cried in distress.

"I'm sorry," said her brother, trying to get up. "Did I break it?" He grabbed his nose. "I guess I broke—it."

"Oh goodness, I hope not," said Holly.

By this time Pete and Pam had run up. Ricky's nose was starting to bleed.

"You'd better go in to mother," Pam advised, pulling out a handkerchief for him. "I'll go with you."

Pete had already unstrapped the toy piano which had some paint scratched off, but otherwise did not seem to be damaged.

Mrs. Hollister, who was making sandwiches in the kitchen, looked at Ricky in alarm. But after she held a cloth of cold water on his nose a few minutes the bleeding stopped.

"I guess moving men have to get hurt sometimes," Ricky said, thanking his pretty blond-haired mother.

Then he ran back to his job.

A few minutes later a station wagon pulled into the driveway and a tall, athletic-looking man stepped out. He had brown eyes which crinkled at the corners when he smiled and brown wavy hair.

"Daddy!" cried Holly, running over. "We're almost moved. When do we start?"

"As soon as Mother's ready," he replied with a smile.

In a short time the Hollister house was empty. The vans were locked up, and the children and their parents stood at the curb to watch them pull away. Just then

"I think I broke – it."

they began to feel a little sad about leaving the old place, where they had had so many good times.

"Why, where's Sue?" Mrs. Hollister asked suddenly, not seeing the little girl.

Sue was nowhere in sight.

"I saw Sue playing with Zip," Ricky said.

Zip was the Hollisters' faithful collie dog, and very much a member of the family.

The children began calling their little sister and whistling for the dog.

"Listen!" Mrs. Hollister commanded, hearing a muffled bark. It seemed to come from the small van.

"Open it," Mr. Hollister ordered.

George quickly flung open the door. Out jumped Zip, barking and wagging his tail, happy to be out of the wagon. Sue climbed down after him.

"I was hiding in Ricky's wagon," said the dark-haired baby of the family, a twinkle in her eyes. "I want to ride in the van. Can't I, please?"

"Not this time," Mrs. Hollister told her.

"Well, I think you're all set now," Mr. Hollister told George. "You fellows will keep right on all night, but we'll stop at a tourist camp somewhere. Be sure to have everything in place for us when we get to Shoreham. This sketch will show how we want things placed in our new home."

He handed a paper of directions to George. The men waved, and the two vans started off.

Now it was time for the Hollisters to leave. The lunch and several suitcases were put into the station

"I was hiding in Ricky's wagon."

wagon, then the old house was locked. Quickly the children scrambled to their places in the car. Sue sat in the front seat with her parents. The other children found their places in the back.

Zip jumped in and curled up on his special cushion. Although Zip loved all the children, he felt that he belonged to Pam. Two years before she had found him hurt in the street. She had adopted the lonely dog and nursed him back to health.

"Oh, look who's coming!" Pam said excitedly.

Running up the street were several boys and girls and two fox terriers.

"I guess they want to say good-by," Mrs. Hollister said, smiling appreciatively.

The dogs began to bark and Zip joined them. He tried to leap out the window, but Pam held on to him with a firm hand.

"Good-by, Holly!" called one little girl. "Be sure to write."

"'By. I'll write as soon as I get there and tell you all about our new house," Holly promised.

"Hey, Pete," called a tall, skinny boy. "If you get any big fish let me know, and I'll come over to visit you." He grinned.

"Sure thing," Pete answered.

There was laughing and shouting as the station wagon pulled out of the driveway and headed out of town. It was late in June. Everything was green and bright. They stopped for lunch by a pretty stream, then continued driving until it was nearly sunset.

"Keep an eye open for a good place to stop for the night," Mr. Hollister said to his family.

"Good-by, Holly!" called one little girl. "Be sure to write."

The children watched eagerly. "I see one!" Pam cried out presently. "It looks pretty."

Mr. Hollister turned into a driveway, at the end of which was a circle of little white cottages with red shutters.

A kindly gray-haired man came out, saying he owned the camp and asked if they would like a place for the night.

"I'll give you my nicest house," he added.

The children were delighted and started at once to help bring in the suitcases.

After a delicious supper, the children and Zip played in front of the cabins. Presently, a boy about Pete's age, tall and heavily built, came from another cottage and walked over. He stood frowning at the Hollisters.

"Hello," Pete said.

The boy did not reply. He stared at them a few seconds longer, then walked off behind the cottages. Zip growled as he watched him go.

"Not a very friendly boy," Pam remarked.

Shortly afterward Holly decided she would take Zip for a run. She went to get his leash from the station wagon. As Holly opened the rear door and stepped inside, she saw the unfriendly boy come from behind a tree.

"What's your name?" he asked gruffly.

"Holly Hollister. What's yours?"

"Joey Brill. Where are you going?"

"To our new home in Shoreham," Holly replied.

"Oh, Joey, don't do that!" Holly cried.

"Shoreham!" the boy exclaimed. "That's where I live. We don't need any more kids in Shoreham. You'll be sorry if you move there."

Holly did not like the rude boy. She wished he would go away. But instead, he came over to the car and stepped into the front seat, and released the brake.

"Oh, Joey, don't do that!" Holly cried. "We'll roll down hill!"

CHAPTER 2
An Attic Secret

"I KNOW how to run a car," Joey bragged, as the station wagon began to move.

When it gained speed, though, he became frightened and tried to pull the brake on. The car slowed a bit, but still it rolled. Joey jumped out. So did Holly. But the station wagon continued to run away.

"Help! Help!" Holly shouted.

Pete heard his sister and saw at a glance what was happening. He raced toward the moving car. Luckily, the station wagon's tailboard had been left down. This was his only chance.

Pete grabbed it as the car rolled by. Quickly he scrambled over the seats and seized the steering wheel.

The car just missed a big tree. Then Pete pulled on the brake and the runaway car skidded to a stop.

"What happened, Holly?" Pete asked, as his sister ran up.

She told him what Joey Brill had done, just as Mr. Hollister and the other children raced up.

Pete was very angry. "Wait 'til I get Joey!" he said, and went off to find him.

This was his only chance.

"Looking for something?" the camp owner asked as he saw Pete searching.

When Pete said he was hunting for Joey, the man replied, "Joey and his parents drove away a few minutes ago."

The man said Joey had come running up, begging his parents to leave at once, because he felt sick. The owner was glad because Joey had been getting into all kinds of mischief since they had come there.

The Hollisters went to bed early that night and rose at sunup next morning to continue their trip. During the afternoon the children grew tired of looking at the scenery and playing all the games which could be played in a car.

"There's a new game in that small suitcase of mine," said their father. "Maybe you children would like to try it. Get it out, Pete."

Mr. Hollister had invented many gadgets and also many toys and games. He always asked his children to try them out before he put them in stores.

"I don't see any small bag, Dad," Pete called.

Ricky suddenly sat up very straight. A frightened look came over his face.

"Daddy," he said, "I put that bag in the little van with our toys. I didn't know you wanted it to go with us."

Mr. Hollister was so amazed he stopped the car. "You—what?"

Ricky became frightened. "The mover asked me if it was to go in the little van and I said yes. But, Daddy, I told him to take extra good care of the bag 'cause it had your inventions in it."

Mr. Hollister started the car. "Well," he sighed, "I suppose everything will be all right. But I would certainly hate to lose that bag."

Presently Pete spied a signpost: *30 Miles to Shoreham.*

"We're practically there!" he shouted.

The children were almost too excited to wait. What did their new home look like? How exciting to be on the shore of a lake!

"What's the name of the lake?" Pam asked.

"Pine Lake," their father replied. "It's a big one, too; has an island in the middle, called Blackberry Island."

The sun had set by the time the Hollisters arrived in Shoreham. How attractive the homes looked!

"Is this our street, Daddy?" asked Sue.

"You guessed it," replied her father. "This is our street, Shoreham Road. Our number is 124."

"And there's our house," shouted Pam. "I know it from the picture the real-estate man sent."

Nestled far back from the road was the Hollisters' new home. It was a large, three-story house. Big lawns stretched away on each side. The lake touched the property in the rear.

Mr. Hollister turned into the pebbly driveway and stopped. "Here we are, children," he said. "Pile out."

The doors of the station wagon were flung open.

"Our furniture has arrived," said Mrs. Hollister, seeing a table through a window.

The children's father went up to the front door, with the others trooping behind him.

"Does he mean all our toys are lost?"

"Look!" said Holly. "There's a note pinned on the door."

Her father read the note aloud. It had been written by George, the driver of the big van, and said:

"It is now six P.M. The small van has not arrived, and the company doesn't know where it is. We have been here since morning and can't wait any longer."

"Does he mean all our toys are lost?" Holly asked fearfully.

"And your bag with the new invention in it!" Pam spoke up.

"I'll go to the police and report this," Mr. Hollister said. "Maybe they've heard something about the missing van by this time."

As soon as he had unlocked the door and looked around the house, he drove off. In the meantime the children hurried from room to room.

"I love it!" Holly cried enthusiastically.

"So do I!" Pam echoed.

The children made their beds, arranged their clothes in the bureau drawers and hung up their suits and dresses in the closets.

Pete and Pam were the speediest. When they finished, they hurried outdoors to look around.

As Holly completed making her bed, she suddenly straightened up. She had heard a strange creaking sound above her. She hurried into the boys' room.

"Listen, Ricky, what's that upstairs?"

Her brother listened. The sound was very faint now.

"I don't know. Nobody's in the attic. Maybe it's a mouse. Let's go up and see."

But Holly thought they should tell their mother, so the children went downstairs to find her.

Meanwhile, Pete and Pam had circled the house, and now stood looking at it. Suddenly Pam gasped and pointed to an attic window.

"Pete, do you see what I see?"

In the dusk she had seen what appeared to be a face. The next moment it disappeared.

"It looked like a man," Pam quavered.

"But how could it be?" Pete argued.

"I guess it couldn't be," Pam agreed. "It might be a dummy or a false face somebody left up there."

"I'll find out," Pete offered.

"I'm going with you," Pam said, and dashed into the house after him and up the stairs.

Pete opened the door to the attic and clicked the light button. But the light did not go on.

"It's sure dark up there," he said. "I'd better get a flashlight."

He hurried to his bedroom and took his flashlight from his dresser. Returning to the dark stairway, he focused its beam upward.

"I'll go first," he told Pam.

Pete tiptoed slowly up the stairs, with his sister directly behind him. When they reached a landing, they stopped to listen. There was not a sound.

Pete went up a few more steps until his head was level with the attic floor. He beamed the light around.

"Maybe somebody was up here," Pam said in a whisper.

The children went up the remaining steps and stood listening.

"It's so spooky up here," Pam said, brushing a cobweb from her face.

"I wonder why the light didn't go on," Pete said.

He directed his flash around to find the fixture. "Oh, I see. There's no bulb in it."

"I'll get one," Pam offered, glad to leave the attic for a minute.

She hurried down to the second floor and took a bulb from a socket in the hall, then returned and screwed it into the fixture. The attic was flooded with light.

"Maybe somebody was up here," Pam said in a whisper.

"Now we can really explore," Pete said.

He opened a closet that had not been noticed before. The door to it squeaked and groaned. The closet was empty.

Next the boy walked over to the window, where Pam had thought she had seen the face.

"Wow!" Pete exclaimed. "Look at this!" and pointed to the sill.

There were finger marks in the dust.

"Somebody was here," Pam said, "but where did he go?"

Pete shrugged. "Let's look around."

He lifted the sash and peered out, but there was no roof beneath the window on which anyone could step. Meanwhile, Pam had found another window. It was open a few inches.

"Maybe the man went out this way," she suggested, and raised herself up to look out. But, like the other window, there was nothing outside to stand on.

As Pam pulled her head in, she noticed something on the floor—the remains of a half-burned match.

"Pete," said his sister, picking up the match, "maybe the man we saw at the window dropped this!"

Their curiosity thoroughly aroused, the two children searched every inch of the attic floor for further clues. A small rug lay near the spot where the brick chimney came up through the floor. Pete tugged at one end of the rug. It did not move.

"It's tacked down," Pam said. "Maybe something's underneath it."

"Maybe something's underneath it."

The boy flashed his light carefully around the edge of the rug. Then he exclaimed:

"Pam, it hides a trap door!"

"How does it open? There's no handle or anything."

"Not even a hinge," Pete sighed.

Then he had an idea. Stepping onto one end of the rug, he saw the door give way a little.

"This is it," Pete shouted. "A trap door on springs."

Pete opened it quickly and flashed his light below. A narrow flight of steps led downward.

"A secret stairway!" Pete gasped. "Our new house has a secret stairway!"

"How wonderful!" Pam cried. Then suddenly she remembered the face at the window. "This may be the way the man left."

"I wonder where the stairs go," said Pete. "I'm going to find out."

"Do you think we should go down alone?" Pam asked. "He might still be around."

Either Pete did not hear her, or else he did not want to wait, for he had already started down, shining his flashlight ahead of him. Pam followed.

Steps, steps, steps! They seemed to go past the second floor, then down past the first floor. Somewhere between the walls the children could dimly hear voices. They must be coming from the kitchen.

Down, down, down the children went. Finally Pete came to a tiny door and pushed. It swung open, and he looked ahead.

"Where are we?" Pam asked.

"I don't know," Pete answered, "but follow me."

CHAPTER 3

A Dog Hero

PAM GRABBED Pete's hand as they stepped down into the darkness. The boy swung his flashlight around. On the front of the door were shelves for food. Nobody would guess it was a door.

"This is our cellar," Pete said. "And look, Pam, that window up there's open. I guess the man went out of it."

"I guess he did," Pam agreed. "There's a box right under it to stand on."

The children found a stairway leading up to the kitchen and pounded on the locked door. Their surprised mother opened it.

"How did you get down there?" she asked.

Pete and Pam excitedly told their story to the family, including their father who had returned from police headquarters.

"Didn't you know about these stairs, Daddy?" Holly asked.

Mr. Hollister said no, the real-estate man had not mentioned them.

"Maybe they're a long, long secret," said Holly, and the others laughed.

Mr. Hollister, though interested in the stairway, whispered to his wife his concern about a possible stranger using it. He wondered what the intruder's reason could be.

"Dad, did you find out anything about the missing van?" Ricky asked hopefully, as the family began their supper.

Mr. Hollister said there was no trace of it yet. "The police are to let me know about it in the morning," he added.

Next day the children were up early. Their father had already left the house.

"Did he go after our toys?" Sue asked.

"No, dear," her mother replied. "To his new store."

"I hope he'll be happy in it," Sue said quaintly.

The Hollisters had moved to Shoreham because of the store. Mr. Hollister had had a chance to buy a hardware business which had closed. To it he had added all kinds of athletic equipment and sporting goods. It would open today.

"I want to see our new store," Holly spoke up.

"We'll go down after a while," her mother promised. "Dad hasn't any clerks yet, so he's going to let you all help him sell the hardware and sporting goods."

"I want to sell boats!" cried Ricky. "And show the people how they work."

While he was waiting for breakfast, Ricky, his mind still on boats, wandered down to their dock. Pete caught up to him.

"Hey, there's our boat," said Ricky. "Let's row it."

The boys looked around, but could not find any oars. Perhaps they were locked in the garage.

"I know what we can do," said Pete. "I'll get out and push the boat. Then I'll pull you in real fast with the rope."

Ricky thought this would be fun. He sat down in the stern and Pete gave the boat a hard push. Away it whizzed. When the boat reached the end of the rope, it swung around hard.

"Oh!" Ricky cried.

He nearly fell into the water but managed to grab the side of the boat just in time. Pete pulled the boat back. Then the boys exchanged places, and Ricky gave Pete a couple of rides.

The boys were so busy playing that they did not notice their little sister Sue walking up the shore. They had last seen her going toward a sandpile in the yard.

He nearly fell into the water.

Sue had built several tunnels and pushed a little stick through, making believe it was a train going into a mountain. But she had tired of this, and decided to walk along the waterfront.

In a few minutes she saw a large rock. Thinking that she could play lighthouse, Sue stepped on top of it. But moss which covered the rock had made it very slippery. Suddenly the little girl's arms flew up, and she lost her balance.

Splash! Sue was in the water. It was not deep, but the water was so cold that the poor child lost her breath and became frightened. She got up but at once fell down again.

None of the Hollisters heard the splash. But Zip did. The collie came bounding across the lawn, jumped into the water, and grabbed Sue's dress in his teeth.

Pete and Ricky had seen Zip racing toward the water. Now they ran over to find out what he was after.

Zip was dragging their little sister from the water!

"Oh!" cried Pete, then added, "Good boy!"

Sue did not know whether to cry or to laugh. Finally she laughed.

"Zip's my bestest friend," she said.

"It's a good thing he was around," Pete told her. "And you'd better stay away from the water, Sue, unless somebody older's with you."

Sue promised. Pete took her back to the house and Pam helped her put on dry clothes.

Ricky forgot all about his flap-jack race.

By this time breakfast was ready. Mrs. Hollister and the children sat down. Their eyes sparkled when they saw what was on the table.

"Flapjacks!" yelled Ricky. "I'll eat ten!"

He was only on his fourth cake when the telephone rang. Mrs. Hollister answered, and the message she received made Ricky forget all about his flapjack race.

"Children," she said, "the police have found the missing van!"

"Hurray! Where?" asked Pam.

"Near Stony Point, a town on the other side of the lake."

"Oh good," said Holly. "Now I can have my little piano."

Mrs. Hollister held up her hand for silence.

"Don't count on getting your toys back," she said. "The police found the van empty."

The children sat stunned for several seconds. Then Ricky said:

"I want to see the van, even if it's empty. Maybe *something's* still in it under those big blankets." His voice quavered. "Maybe Daddy's suitcase."

Mrs. Hollister thought a moment, then decided they would go. The children's father had left the station wagon at home. Quickly the food was put away, and the dishes placed into the dishwasher. Then they started for Stony Point.

"Mother," said Pete, "do you think that strange man Pam and I saw in our attic had anything to do with the van?"

"I wonder," she replied. "Certainly we've had plenty of mystery since coming to our new home."

"But we're going to stay happy, aren't we?" asked Sue, who was never sad very long.

"Of course," her mother replied. "The Hollisters won't let this keep them from smiling."

However, she was concerned about her husband's lost invention.

Just before they reached the town, the Hollisters saw a police car with two officers in it alongside the road. Mrs. Hollister stopped and told them who she was.

"The van is on that little side road," one of the officers said, pointing.

The children got out and ran to it. The van had a flat tire, the back doors were open, and there was nothing inside, not even a blanket.

"Strangest thing I ever saw," said the policeman, coming up with Mrs. Hollister. "I don't know where the stuff disappeared to. We followed some tracks into the woods but that's as far as we got."

The children looked downhearted. The toys had vanished and so had the special suitcase. They got back into the station wagon and headed for their father's store in Shoreham. All of them were quiet—they had lost their jolly chatter and gay smiles because they felt very sad about losing all their toys.

"I suppose we'll have to wait until Christmas for new ones," said Holly glumly.

To make them happy again, Mrs. Hollister suggested that they might earn a little money helping their father, and perhaps buy some simple toys.

There was nothing inside.

"There's the store," she said, stopping on the main street of town. "Isn't it nice?"

The children gasped. They had not expected to see such a good-looking shop with big show windows and a fine display of merchandise.

"The new name's painted on!" cried Pete excitedly, *"The Trading Post!"*

As the children entered the store and saw the attractively filled shelves, they set up a cheer. How exciting to have a chance to be real storekeepers!

While Mrs. Hollister told her husband about the empty van, the children explored *The Trading Post.* What *ohs* and *ahs* came from them as they looked around the wonderful store. A new water cooler stood beside the door, on the side of a long aisle, which ran down the middle of the store.

On the left side were all sorts of sporting goods—fishing tackle, roller skates, baseball bats, and tennis rackets. Beyond this section were toys.

On the right side was the hardware department—hammers and nails, saws, wires and cans of paint.

"This is going to be fun, Dad," said Ricky, as three customers walked in.

Mr. Hollister went to wait on them, with the children helping. One man bought a pound of nails. A woman took an orange squeezer, and remarked with a twinkle in her eye that she would like to squeeze little Sue, too.

Sue thought the woman meant it, and scooted to the other side of the store. There she found a black and white rocking horse which just fit her.

"I'm going to catch you, Sue!"

"How 'dorable," she said aloud, as she sat down on it and began to rock back and forth. "I'm going to be a cowboy girl."

This idea intrigued Ricky, who was always playing cowboys and Indians. If Sue could be a cowgirl, that would be wonderful. Ricky found a piece of rope. Making a loop in one end, he fashioned a lasso.

"I'm going to catch you, Sue!" he said, twirling the rope.

"I'm going to put some of that energy of yours to work," Mr. Hollister called to Ricky. "Suppose you help unpack a carton of doll furniture."

Eagerly Ricky followed his father to a side door, which opened onto a driveway. A truckman was unloading a big box. He carried it inside and set it down alongside a tall stack of bait cans.

Ricky, Pete and Pam went to work ripping open the carton. Inside were all kinds of bright-colored doll tables, chairs, refrigerators and swings.

"This is fun," Pam exclaimed as she carefully unpacked each piece.

The children were so busy that they did not notice the side door open quietly. A boy slipped into the store without making a sound. When nobody was looking, he sneaked up behind the stack of cans.

Suddenly the stack began to move. It tilted over farther and farther. Then with a crunching sound the whole pile toppled over toward the three Hollister children.

"Look out!" a voice across the store shouted.

CHAPTER 4

A Wonderful Party

HEARING THE cry, Pete and Pam looked up. The tall pile of cans was about to fall on their heads!

The children jumped to one side as the cans clattered to the floor. Mr. and Mrs. Hollister and the customers came running over to see what had happened and who had cried out the warning.

"I guess I shouted just in time," said an elderly man who now stood near the children. He was tall and thin and had twinkling eyes.

"Thank you," said Mr. Hollister. "Ricky, Pete, and Pam might have been injured. I can't understand what made the cans topple over."

"A boy pushed them," said the stranger. "I don't know who he was, but I saw him run out that side door."

At mention of the word, *boy*, Pete dashed out the side door and up the driveway to the street. He saw a boy disappearing around a corner. Pete tried to catch up to him, but lost sight of him.

"Maybe he was Joey," Pete thought. "I'll find out some time."

When he returned to the store, the cans had been picked up. The old man was talking to Mr. Hollister.

The tall pile of cans was about to fall.

He said he was Roy Tinker, but that everybody called him just Tinker. He used to work at *The Trading Post*, before he had been hit by a car and gone to the hospital.

"Hm," said Mr. Hollister, looking about the store. More customers were coming in. "How would you like to work for me?"

When Tinker said he would, the children were pleased. What a nice man to have at *The Trading Post!*

Mr. Hollister said Tinker could drive the store's small truck, as well as wait on customers. Tinker thanked him and immediately went to help the people.

During the afternoon, Pete sold some tools, and Rick and Holly, several games. Pam was busy at the seed counter. Even little Sue helped by selling some doll's clothespins to a little girl.

"This is lots of fun," said Pam as they were about to close the store for the evening. "More fun than just playing store. I'm so glad we have *The Trading Post*—and Tinker—and our new home, too!"

"Three cheers for the Happy Hollisters!" called out Tinker, catching their enthusiasm.

When the children arrived home, they found five little envelopes all alike waiting for them.

"What are these?" asked Pam.

"Something nice," Mrs. Hollister answered, smiling.

Eagerly, the five of them tore open their first mail at their new home. Holly was the first to read hers.

"An invitation!" she cried. "An invitation to a party!"

As each child read his invitation, he gave a shout of joy. The letters had been sent by Jeff and Ann Hunter, who lived down the street. The party was to introduce the Hollister children to their new neighbors, and would be held tomorrow afternoon at two o'clock.

The next day all of them arrived promptly. Jeff and Ann opened the door. Jeff was eight years old. He had dark straight hair and blue eyes, and looked like his sister. Only Ann, who was ten, had curly hair that hung in ringlets. Her long black lashes made her gray eyes look large and pretty, and she had deep dimples when she laughed.

Pam knew immediately that she had found a new friend and was very happy. She introduced herself and her brothers and sisters to Mrs. Hunter and said the Hollisters were very pleased to have been invited.

"I'm delighted that such a nice family has moved into the big house," Mrs. Hunter smiled.

While Jeff was showing Ricky his playroom, Dave Mead arrived. He was twelve years old and had tousled hair. He lived three doors from the Hollisters. Right away he and Pete began to talk about the lake and fishing and sailboats.

Holly wondered if there would be any girls her age. No sooner had she thought this, when Donna Martin ran in. Donna was seven. She was plump and had a dimple in each cheek.

"I'm glad you moved here," she said to Holly. "Would you like to come over and play with my doll house sometime?"

Pam knew immediately that she had found a new friend.

How jolly everybody was! A few more children arrived, and then the doorbell gave a long ring.

"I wonder who that is?" Ann said, as she hurried to answer the bell.

The children heard a loud voice at the door.

"I'm here!"

Joey Brill! The Hollister children gasped.

And Joey gasped when he saw them! "How'd you get here?" he asked rudely.

"We were invited," Pam answered.

"Huh! The Hunters sure took a chance asking you," Joey said. "Nobody knows who you are."

Mrs. Hunter stepped forward. "Joey, if you can't act nice, you may leave."

"All right!"

"Does Joey live near here?" Holly whispered to Donna.

"Just around the corner," Donna answered. "Nobody likes him. He's always making trouble."

"Then why was he invited?" Holly asked.

Ann heard her and said, "Mother's very kind. She's always hoping Joey will behave himself."

At first Joey Brill did. But after he had been quiet for a few minutes, he began to argue with Pete.

"I'll bet I can throw a ball farther'n you can," he said, "and row a boat faster, and swim underwater better, too!"

"We'll wait and see," replied Pete quietly.

Pam took Ann Hunter aside. "Is Joey always bragging like that?" she asked.

Joey landed in Ricky's lap.

"Yes," said Ann. "That's one of the reasons why nobody likes him."

The children played games for nearly two hours. Mrs. Hunter helped while they played musical chairs. Joey was put out of the game early when Ricky slipped into a seat ahead of him, and Joey landed in Ricky's lap.

"I guess you thought I was Pam," Ricky giggled. "Why would you want to sit on a boy's lap?"

Joey shouted, "Be quiet." Then he gave Ricky a hard shove.

"Stop that, Joey," Mrs. Hunter said sternly. Joey glowered and went off into a corner.

Holly won the game and was given a prize which was a tiny doll with a lacy dress. She hugged her tightly.

"I'm going to name her Ann after you," she told Ann Hunter.

After that the children trooped outside. There were slides and swings, and they had fun on them for twenty minutes.

Then Mrs. Hunter called them to the porch, where tables and chairs were set up. The children came running and sat down at their places.

There was a big dish of ice cream and cake at each place, along with a little favor. The children opened their favors, which contained little hats and papers on which were printed their fortunes. They giggled as each one in turn read aloud something funny about himself.

"Listen to mine," said Donna Martin.

"If you'll find a tail and swing from a tree,
You can easily be a little monkey."

Finally when it was Holly's turn, Joey Brill, who was sitting next to her, leaned over to look at the fortune.

"I can read it myself," said Holly.

"If you have a neighbor quite contrary,
My guess is that her name is Mary."

"Mary, Mary," laughed several of the children, pointing at Joey Brill. "Joey's name is Mary."

Joey became very angry. He wanted to hit somebody, but did not dare. Holly was giggling so hard, she had to put her head down until her nose was almost touching the ice cream.

Suddenly, Joey had an idea. He pushed Holly's head down right into the ice cream!

Joey jumped up from the table and ran for the door. Pete instantly set off after him. He gained on the mean boy as they raced across the lawn. Then, with a flying tackle, he tumbled Joey to the ground. The boys rolled over and over as the other children from the party gathered around them.

"Give it to him good!" cried Dave.

When the fighters scrambled to their feet, Joey punched Pete, and Pete hit him back. Finally Mrs. Hunter reached the scene.

"Stop! Stop!" she cried, separating the boys. Then she gave Joey a scolding.

With a flying tackle, he tumbled Joey to the ground.

The boy scowled. "It's all their fault," he said. "The Hollisters think they can come to our town and do anything they want. Who cares about the Hollisters, anyhow? Their house is haunted."

With that Joey hurried away. Pete turned to Jeff. "Haunted? Is our house haunted?"

All the children began to answer at the same time, each one with a different story. Finally Pete got them to talk one at a time.

"I heard," declared Jeff, "that a rich old man who built your house hid a lot of money in it. Then he forgot where he put it."

"No wonder," continued Dave. "He built a lot of secret places in it. Anybody might forget where he hid a treasure in a house like that."

Pam did not really believe all this, and said so. But Donna added:

"Our laundress says the old man walks in his sleep and goes to your house at night to find the lost treasure."

The Hollisters did not know what to believe. When the party was over, they hurried home to tell their mother about the mystery. She did not seem the least bit worried.

"Nonsense," she said. "There is no such thing as a haunted house. Besides, the man who built this house is a very nice old gentleman. He lives on the other side of town with his daughter."

"Then he'd have a long way to walk in his sleep, wouldn't he?" Ricky chuckled. "Do you suppose he uses a sleep-walking map?"

"If our house isn't haunted," Holly spoke up, "why did we hear those funny noises?"

Pam was not convinced either. "What about the face in the attic window?"

Mrs. Hollister said that everything could no doubt be explained, and that they should not fret about it.

"Now go outside and play until bedtime," she said, smiling.

Next morning Pete decided to find out more about the story of the hidden treasure. He would ask the grown-up neighbors what they knew about it. He spoke to several of his new friends' parents.

The stories were all the same. The old man who had owned the house had never caused any trouble, but he was queer. He chased away children who came on his property, and rarely spoke to the neighbors. But no one knew exactly what the treasure was nor where it was hidden.

"If there ever was one, he probably took it with him," Mrs. Smith said.

Pete had been so busy inquiring that before he realized it, he was half a mile from his home. He was about to turn back when suddenly he spied a little girl pushing a doll carriage. It looked familiar. His sister had had one just like it.

Could this be Sue's stolen carriage?

CHAPTER 5

A Funny Little Hat

WALKING UP to the little girl, Pete asked her if he could look at the underside of the carriage. When she said he could, Pete turned it over. There, burned into the wood, were two initials, "S.H."

Sue Hollister! It was her doll carriage!

As Pete set it upright, the little girl's older brother approached.

"Where did you get this carriage?" Pete asked.

There, burned into the wood, were two initials.

"We got it this morning for my sister's birthday," the boy answered.

"You bought it?"

"Yes, at the secondhand store in town."

Pete asked where the store was. When the boy gave him the address, Pete hurried off toward the center of Shoreham. The secondhand shop was only a block from *The Trading Post*.

Pete walked in and introduced himself to the stout proprietor.

"And what can I do for you, sonny?" the man asked.

Pete told him about the empty van and how he had discovered Sue's stolen doll carriage.

"Oh dear," the man said, "this is terrible. If I had known it was stolen, I never would have bought it."

"Who sold it to you?" Pete asked.

The shopkeeper said he had purchased the carriage from a stranger, who was dressed in rather rough clothes.

"What did he look like?" Pete asked.

The storekeeper scratched his head. "Well, the only thing I can remember about him is that he wore a funny little hat."

"I guess you'll have to get the carriage back for my sister," Pete said.

The storekeeper readily agreed. He kept on saying how sorry he was, as they went together to the home of the little girl.

When they reached the house, the secondhand man rang the bell and the little girl's mother appeared. Pete spoke to her.

"My sister's doll carriage was sold to you by mistake," he said.

At first the woman did not know what he was talking about. Then the man explained that he had bought a stolen carriage and would have to return it to its rightful owner.

The child's mother was reluctant to give up the carriage, but when the dealer told her it was against the law to sell stolen goods, she readily accepted the money she had paid.

"If I ever see that man again," said the storekeeper in a threatening tone of voice, "I'll tell the police."

"And please let us know too," Pete said. "He probably has our other things that were stolen from the van."

Pete felt a little silly pushing a doll carriage along the street. He was even more embarrassed when he met Joey.

"Ho, ho!" Joey cried. "Sissy Hollister plays with dolls!"

Pete flushed but went on. He pushed the carriage the rest of the way home. How happy Sue was to see him!

"My dolly needs fresh air," she said affectionately, running into the house to get Annie, the only doll she had now.

Ricky, who was climbing a pear tree to see about building a tree hut, and Pam, who was watching him, came running to find out about the carriage. When Pete told his story, the children became excited and wanted to go find the man with the funny hat at once.

But Mrs. Hollister said they must not wander around the town. After she had gone indoors, Pete said:

"Pam, let's hunt for the treasure the fellows said might be hidden in our house."

"Sure," she said eagerly. "But where?"

"It's probably somewhere along the secret staircase," Pete guessed.

The two children got a flashlight, went to the cellar and opened the door to the secret stairs. Using the light, they examined the stairway clear to the top and then down to the bottom again.

"I guess there's nothing here," Pete said, discouraged.

Pam leaned back against the wall to rest. As she did, her hand touched a tiny button concealed in the wall. There was a sound like the clicking of a little spring.

"Oh!" Pam exclaimed, as the wall back of her began to move. "What's this?"

Pete flashed the light on the wall. A small door had swung in toward the chimney. The children peered beyond.

"A tiny room," Pam whispered.

She and Pete explored the room, which was no larger than a small closet and had no windows.

"If there was ever any treasure here," Pete said, "it's been taken away by this time."

When they showed their discovery to the rest of the family, they, too, were baffled about the little room. What could it have been used for?

After the Hollister family went to bed that night, everything was peaceful and quiet. Even Zip, who had

The wall back of her began to move.

chased frogs near the water's edge all day, was sleeping soundly in the kitchen.

But in the middle of the night there came a strange sound. Zip was the first one to hear the faint but disturbing noise. He barked loudly and ran around the kitchen.

Pete awakened and slipped into his father's room. Mr. Hollister was up.

"Dad, do you suppose the person we saw at the window is making that noise?"

"If he is," Mr. Hollister said grimly, "we're going to catch him!"

Together they hurried downstairs. Zip was still barking and scratching on the cellar door. Mr. Hollister opened it, switched on the light, and walked cautiously down the stairs, his son behind him.

Nobody was in sight. The two looked in every possible hiding place. Then Mr. Hollister opened the door to the secret stair. While Pete peeked into the secret room, Mr. Hollister flashed his light and walked to the top floor.

When he came down, he reported that no one was there either. Then Pete tried the cellar door which led into the yard. It was locked, but there was something very strange about it.

"Look, Dad," he called.

Mr. Hollister came over.

"The door is locked, but the key is on the outside," Pete explained.

Somebody had been in the cellar! Whoever it was had left by that door and had locked it from the outside, probably to delay his pursuers.

Mr. Hollister bolted the cellar door and left the door to the kitchen open so that Zip could take care of anybody who might come into the cellar.

At breakfast, the other children were amazed to hear what had happened.

"Well," Mr. Hollister said, "he's a real live ghost, and he's going to be hard to catch. However, there is nothing we can do unless he returns."

Later in the morning Pam and Holly went down to the lake front.

"Let's go out in the rowboat," Holly suggested.

Mr. Hollister opened the door to the secret stair.

"We mustn't go far," warned Pam. "Where are the oars?"

"I'll get them," her sister offered and raced toward the garage. Soon she was back with the oars and jumped into the boat.

"Let me row?" she asked.

"Go ahead," said Pam, "but only in shallow water, Mother said."

Pam untied the rope which held the boat to the dock, and then shoved off. Holly was not very skillful at rowing and splashed the oars up and down. Pam had to keep dodging so the water from them would not soak her. Before they knew it, the girls were in deeper water.

"Oh, see that big black cloud!" cried Holly, looking up.

"It's going to rain," shouted Pam. "We'd better get back to shore."

Holly had often seen Pete whirl the boat around fast by holding one oar in the water and rowing hard with the other. She would try this.

But as she did so, both oars slipped from her hands. They jerked clear out of the oarlocks and landed in the water. Before Pam could grab them, they had drifted away from the boat.

"Oh dear," wailed Holly, "what'll we do?"

Pam knew she must not become panicky. "We'll paddle with our hands," she decided in desperation.

The two girls started to paddle this way as fast as they could. But by this time a strong wind had begun to blow, moving the boat farther and farther from shore. The girls cried for help, but their voices were lost in the strong gale.

Soon they were in the middle of the lake, with whitecaps slapping at the side of the boat. Then the shore of Blackberry Island came into sight. The wind was blowing them right toward it! When the rowboat touched the shore, Pam hopped out and helped Holly up on the pebbly beach.

"Oh, I'm glad we're here," said Holly with a sigh of relief. "But how'll we get home?"

"Just wait for somebody to come and rescue us," Pam answered hopefully.

The oars jerked clear out of the oarlocks.

After a slight sprinkle of rain, the storm cloud passed over, and the wind died down. Pam took Holly's hand, and they walked along the shore together.

"Do you suppose anybody lives here?" Holly asked her sister.

"Daddy said there used to be a farmhouse on this island once," Pam replied, "but nobody lives in it now."

"Somebody's been here today," Holly said. "Look!"

She pointed to a group of loose stones in the sand. It was a crude fireplace with a few blackened embers. There was still warmth in them.

As Pam stared in wonder, she made a startling discovery. Alongside the campfire, half torn and soaked with water, was a picture of the Hollisters' house!

"It's just like the one the real-estate man sent Daddy," Holly said. "How'd it get here?"

Pam said perhaps the real-estate man had come there on a picnic and dropped it. She put the picture in her pocket.

It was not long before Holly forgot that they were stranded on Blackberry Island because she became interested in the beautiful pebbles on the beach. Some were white with pink candy-striped lines on them.

"They look like little Easter eggs!" Holly cried in delight. She scooped up a dozen of them. "I'm going to take these home to mother."

Pam said nothing but she was beginning to worry. No one was in sight on the lake.

Holly wandered off to gather more stones. Soon she saw some colored ones on the far side of a large puddle, a short distance from shore.

The little girl was sure she could jump across the puddle, but when she tried she landed in the middle of it. In a moment her feet began to sink in the sandy mud. Holly struggled to free herself, but the more she struggled, the deeper she sank.

"Pam, come quick! I'm sinking!" she cried out.

CHAPTER 6

A Family of Pets

Pam raced along the shore to Holly's side.

"Don't move!" she ordered. "That makes it worse."

She looked for a board to lay across the puddle in order to reach her sister. None was in sight. Then Pam remembered the campfire a distance up the beach. There had been some broken boards beside it.

Running there as fast as she could, Pam picked up a long one and hurried back to her sister. Poor Holly was up to her waist!

"I'll have you out in a minute," Pam promised.

She placed the board across the deep puddle and walked out on it. She could not budge Holly.

Pam had to do something quickly!

She saw a thick tangle of vines a little distance from the shore and went to tear them up. Quickly she wove them into a braid.

"Oh, I'll never get out!" Holly wailed.

"Yes, you will," Pam said with determination.

She fashioned a loop in one end of the vine rope and threw it over her sister's head.

"Put it under your arms," she said.

The rope kept her from sinking deeper.

Holly did this and Pam pulled. Holly did not rise, but at least the rope kept her from sinking deeper.

Soon Pam's arms began to ache. She could not pull any more. Walking back a few steps to where an old rotted tree trunk stuck out of the ground, she tied the other end of the vine rope around the trunk while she rested.

Holly had stopped crying, though tears still glistened in her eyes.

"I won't go down through the earth all the way to China," she said bravely.

As Pam looked imploringly over the lake for help, suddenly she cried out: "Look! A motorboat!"

It was too far out to see for sure who was in it. But as the bobbing boat came close to shore, Holly exclaimed:

"It's Dad and Pete. They've borrowed a boat!"

In a few minutes the craft touched the shore. As Pete tied the boat's rope to a tree, his father raced up to his daughters. Pam was still tugging on the vine rope. She was nearly exhausted.

"Hold on tight!" Mr. Hollister called to her encouragingly and grabbed hold of the vines. He tugged hard and pulled Holly out of the mud.

"You saved your sister's life," he praised Pam. "Now tell me what happened."

As Pam and the others wiped some of the mud from Holly, she told the story of the drifting boat and how her sister had become mired.

"How did you know where to find us?" she asked.

Pete said they had found the oars, and then the wind had given them a clue to where the rowboat might have drifted.

All this time Holly had been looking at her muddy playclothes. "I know what I'll do," she said. "I'll take a bath with everything on."

Mr. Hollister laughed. "I guess that's the best thing to do," he said, as she started for the shore of the lake.

Both girls took off their shoes and socks, and Pam held Holly's hand as they trotted into the lake. After a few minutes of splashing around, all the mud was washed from her clothes.

"Suppose we walk along the beach in the sun so you can dry off, Holly," Mr. Hollister suggested.

They set out along the beach. About a quarter of a mile away they could see the tumbledown remains of an old farmhouse.

"What a spooky looking place!" said Holly in a scared voice, as they approached it.

The roof had sagged, most of the shingles had fallen off, and the porch hung down in front of the house like a broken arm. The yard was so overgrown with blackberry bushes, that Pete's legs and arms were badly scratched as he went near the house.

"Crickets!" he moaned. "Now I know why they call this place Blackberry Island."

"I think it should be called Stickery Island," Holly laughed. "I'm dry now. Let's go home."

They turned back. Before climbing into the motorboat, Pete tied their rowboat to the stern of it. Soon the outboard motor was purring, and they started across the lake. The other Hollisters were on the dock to meet them.

"I hear it, too," she said excitedly.

"Holly! Pam!" their mother exclaimed with relief in her voice. "You're safe!"

The story was quickly told, and then the girls went to take baths before eating supper.

When the children went to bed that night, Zip followed Pete to his room and bounded up on the bed. He was asleep before Pete. In the middle of the night, the boy heard him stir and whine. Pete sat upright.

The prowler again? Pete listened intently as he went into the hall. There he met Pam.

"I—I hear it, too," she said excitedly. "It sounds like somebody crying. Maybe it's Sue."

They tiptoed into her room to see if she was ill or dreaming, as she sometimes cried out in her sleep. But she lay in her bed sound asleep. Where could the cries be coming from?

The children listened again.

"It's coming from downstairs," Pam said. "Let's go see what it is."

"All right."

They tiptoed down the stairs, with Zip padding behind them. Pete put his hand on the dog's head, which was his way of showing the faithful collie that he must not bark.

"Sh!" he whispered. "Don't make any noise."

When they reached the kitchen, the crying sound became louder. Pam opened the cellar door.

"It's coming from down there," she said.

Pete switched on the light. Together the children went down the stairs.

"Listen," Pete said, "the noise is coming from over in that corner."

As they approached the place, Pam squealed, but not in fear.

"Pete, look! Kittens! Aren't they darling?"

On a piece of burlap bag lay a mother cat and five kittens. Pam had seen very young kittens before. These seemed to be about three weeks old.

Pete looked up and saw that the cellar window was partly open.

"That's how they got in," he observed. "I wonder where they came from?"

Suddenly the children heard footsteps above them. Mr. and Mrs. Hollister came down the stairs, followed by Holly and Ricky.

"Kittens! We've found kittens!" Pam cried happily. "A mother and five children."

"The Hollister cat family," said Holly, "and there's one for each of us."

The little girl came nearer and stooped down to pat the tiny animals, but as she did so, the mother cat hissed.

"Stay away from them, dear," Mrs. Hollister said. "The mother doesn't know yet that we are friendly. She is only trying to protect her babies."

The Hollisters decided to leave them there for the night. Pete shut the window so the cats could not get out. The family trooped back to bed, but remained awake a while.

"We've found kittens!" Pam cried.

Little Holly was full of ideas. The next day she would make doll clothes for the cats. She would dress them up, and perhaps have a cat puppet show.

Ricky had ideas, too. He would have a cat parade, and march them around the house. Perhaps he could make little collars for the cats, and put little flags in the collars. Finally all the children fell asleep dreaming of cats.

Next morning they were up earlier than usual. What excitement there was as they rushed down to the cellar to see the cats!

They were friendly now. The mother cat was licking her babies, and she did not hiss at her visitors.

"I know what I'm going to call the mother cat," Holly said. "White Nose."

Ricky wanted to call the black kitten Midnight. There was a white one which Pam named Snowball. The little one with all mixed colors, Pete thought, should be called Tutti-Frutti, and the gray one Holly named Smoky. They could not think of a name for the fifth kitten, but when it snuggled under his mother, Sue said:

"Let's call him Cuddly."

"I think this is even better than finding a treasure in the house," Holly cooed. "I just love cats."

At the breakfast table, Mrs. Hollister suggested that the children try to find the owner of the cats. Perhaps they belonged to some child who would be sad that they had left.

"I think the mother cat is a wild one," said Ricky.

"Or perhaps," Pete added, "she had a cruel master and ran away from home."

It was not long before word of the Hollisters' new cat family spread around the neighborhood. Donna Martin was the first of their playmates to come in to see them. How she wished she had five little kittens!

Then Ann Hunter came over with her brother, Jeff. Later, when Dave Mead came in to see White Nose and her kittens, he ran his hand through his tousled hair, and said:

"You know, this looks like Joey Brill's old cat. She disappeared about a month ago."

"Ugh!" grunted Ricky. "I don't blame her."

The children were upset to hear that the cat might belong to the boy. Pam told her mother about this possibility.

"Well, if it's Joey's cat," she pointed out, "I think you had better find out, and return her to him."

"Maybe he was mean to White Nose," Pam said.

Mrs. Hollister explained that if the cat were Joey's property, he had a right to her. Perhaps he would treat White Nose better so she wouldn't run away again.

The children talked it over, and agreed that their mother was right. But before they had a chance to call on Joey, they saw the boy walking down the street. Donna had told him about White Nose.

"Where's my cat?" he demanded as he approached the Hollister children.

"We don't know that it's your cat," Pete replied defensively. "But if it is, I guess you can have her back."

"That's my cat," he shouted.

They led Joey Brill down into the cellar.

"That's my cat," he shouted. "She's been missing for weeks, and now she has a family. I'm going to take her and all the kittens."

CHAPTER 7

An Exciting Stunt

"OH NO, you can't," said Holly. "You can have White Nose, but you can't have the kittens."

"Why can't I?"

"Did you lose the kittens, too?" Holly asked.

"Well, no," Joey admitted.

Holly smiled. "Then you can only have what you lost," said the little girl.

The other children had never thought of this, but it did seem to make sense. Joey reluctantly agreed to take the cat and leave the kittens. He told the children that White Nose's other name was Buttermilk.

"Come on, Buttermilk," he coaxed, "we're going home." But the cat did not move.

"See," said Ricky, "she doesn't want to go with you. She wants to stay with her kittens."

"I'm going to take her anyway," said Joey.

He glanced around the cellar and saw an old basket with a cover. Then Joey reached down and grabbed the cat around the middle. The angry cat scratched and meowed, but Joey pushed her roughly into the basket, slammed the cover down and sat on it.

"Now I have you," he said triumphantly. "You're not going to get away from me again."

"What are you going to do with her?" Pam asked.

"Lock her in our storage room," Joey replied. "That will teach her not to run off."

The Hollister children felt very sorry for White Nose and her kittens. The babies were big enough to stay away from their mother, although no one would have thought so the way White Nose scratched and cried inside the basket.

The children opened the cellar door for Joey. He carried the cat out into the back yard. She was still crying and scratching.

"I think I know what I'll do to her," Joey said. "I'm going to cool her off in the lake."

"But cats don't like water," Pam pleaded.

"I'll make this one like water," Joey said.

Then the boy went out onto the end of the dock, and lowered the basket into the water.

The cat did not like this treatment one bit. When the water was near the top of the basket, the lid suddenly flew off.

The cat sprang out and scratched Joey's hand. As the boy jumped back to get out of the way, he tripped on the dock.

"Catch him, catch him!" shouted Pam to Pete, who was near him.

But it was too late. With a big splash, Joey Brill fell over backwards into the water. He went completely

With a big splash, Joey Brill fell in.

under, then struggled to the surface. Pete reached down and helped him back onto the dock.

"That cat! Where's that cat?" Joey shouted.

White Nose, who was no more in favor of a dunking than was Joey, had scampered up to the topmost branches of a high tree.

"You Hollisters are going to pay for this!" he shouted, as he stomped off toward his home.

When he was out of sight, White Nose came down cautiously out of the tree. With her tail high in the air, she pranced across the lawn like a drum majorette, and walked to the cellar door. Holly let her in. The kittens mewed when they saw their mother, and Holly brought them a bowl of milk.

At noontime Mr. Hollister returned for lunch. Now that he had Tinker broken in as a storekeeper, he often came home at twelve o'clock to eat. Today Mr. Hollister seemed to have something on his mind.

"Are you thinking up a new invention, Dad?" Pete asked.

"Not exactly, son. I'm trying to think of a way to get more business for *The Trading Post*."

"Isn't business good?" asked Pam.

"Yes, it's good," her father replied. "But I'm going to have to do a lot more business if I want to make a real success of my store."

Mrs. Hollister smiled at her husband and said, "What is your idea for getting more customers at *The Trading Post*?"

"We have to figure out some sort of a stunt," said Mr. Hollister. "Something to advertise the place."

Holly spoke up. "I have an idea. Why couldn't we write letters to everybody in town, telling them what a wonderful place *The Trading Post* is?"

Mr. Hollister thought the idea was pretty good, but sometimes people did not read advertisements.

"This has to be something spectacular," Mr. Hollister said.

"What is a speck on a tackler, Daddy?" said Sue.

All the children laughed, and her father explained to his little girl that spectacular meant exciting, like putting on a little circus in your back yard.

"Then let's have a little circus," said Sue eagerly.

The word "circus" suddenly made a plan click in Pete's mind. He snapped his fingers.

"Circus balloons. Why couldn't we have a stunt with balloons?" he asked.

While the rest of the family listened intently, Pete outlined his plan. The Hollisters would blow up a lot of balloons. In three of them they would put a slip of paper which would say:

"At *The Trading Post* you will receive a prize."

Then all of the balloons would be dropped off a high steeple of a church in the center of town. Naturally, all the children would rush for the balloons.

"And let the air out to see who's lucky," said Holly.

"No, they have to bring them to the store blown up," Pete declared. "That'll make everyone go to *The Trading Post* to see who has the lucky numbers."

"I think that's a dandy idea," said Pam. "What do you think, Daddy?"

Mr. Hollister agreed. He would advertise the scheme in the newspaper and bring home a big box of balloons from *The Trading Post*. That night the children could blow up the balloons for the grand stunt.

That afternoon Pete telephoned the sexton of the old church. He said he would be very glad to let the children drop balloons from halfway up the steeple.

When Mr. Hollister brought the balloons home that night, the whole house buzzed with excitement. Pam wrote many little slips of paper. Each one said:

"Buy your toys at *The Trading Post*."

But on three special ones, it also said:

"This is a lucky number balloon. *The Trading Post* has a prize for you."

Ricky, Holly and Pete were blowing up the balloons.

While Pam was doing this, Ricky, Holly and Pete were blowing up the balloons. Some were round, others were long. They came in all sizes and were red, yellow, white, green and blue.

Before bedtime all the balloons were ready. Pam counted them. There were a hundred and two. The children tied short strings to each balloon and held them in bunches like the balloon men at the circuses.

Just as they were finishing their job, Pete glanced toward the window. He saw a head bob quickly out of sight.

"Who's there?" he called.

There was no reply as Pete hurried to look out. It was dark and quiet.

"Maybe it's the old man walking in his sleep," Ricky said with a grin. "Let's invite him in and give him a balloon."

"Don't be silly," Holly scolded. "It might have been just a shadow."

In order to make certain it was not a prowler, Pete ran out the back door and looked around the house. He could see nobody. Then he came back inside and helped the others put the balloons in one corner of the living room.

Early the next morning, word quickly spread among the children about the Hollister balloons.

"When are you going to drop them?" Dave Mead wanted to know.

"At one o'clock this afternoon," Pam replied.

After lunch Mr. Hollister drove the children and the balloons to *The Trading Post*.

"What are the prizes going to be?" Ricky asked.

"I haven't decided that yet," Mr. Hollister replied. "What do you think would make good prizes?"

Ricky said a pair of roller skates. Then Holly suggested a doll, if a girl should win. Pam thought a tennis racket might be nice.

"All right," their father agreed. "Those will be the three prizes."

What excitement there was as the time drew near to drop the balloons! It was arranged that Pete and Pam should take them up to the opening in the steeple. Ricky and Holly begged to go along. They wanted to see the town of Shoreham from high up.

"If you promise to be careful, you may go," Mr. Hollister said.

At ten minutes to one, the four children set off for the church. They were met at the door by the sexton, who led them up a long stairway.

The children carried so many balloons in their hands that they could hardly see ahead of them. The balloons bounced against their faces, and they were very glad when they reached the little balcony.

"The children down there look just like dolls," Pam said, glancing at the crowd of excited boys and girls.

Finally the hand of the big clock in the church steeple pointed to one o'clock. The bell went *bong*.

"Let 'em go!" Pete shouted.

He and Pam released the balloons, amid the shouts of the children below. The balloons scattered in all directions as the wind carried them up and down and sideways. The Hollisters watched for a moment as their little friends made a mad scramble for them.

What a scene! Traffic was stopped completely as the children ran here and there, jumping and grabbing to get the bobbing balloons.

"I think we'd better get back to *The Trading Post*," Pete said. "The kids'll be coming in soon."

Many of the children's parents had accompanied them to town to watch the fun. Now they all started to enter *The Trading Post*.

As each balloon was presented to Mr. Hollister, he opened it carefully and took out the little slips of paper. Finally, so many children came in all at once that Pete

"Let 'em go!" Pete shouted.

and Pam had to help him, while Roy Tinker took care of grown-up customers.

Presently a little boy named Phil held up his balloon to Pete, who opened it and read the paper.

"Here's a lucky number!" said Pete.

"Yippee!" yelled Phil. Everybody gathered around the boy.

"What would you like to have, roller skates or a tennis racket?" Mr. Hollister asked.

"Roller skates!" He picked them out.

After the Hollisters had let the air out of about fifty balloons, Ann Hunter rushed in. "I found this one over by the lake," she said breathlessly.

Pam opened it. Another lucky number!

"Oh, Ann, I'm so glad you won," Pam said.

"Well, young lady, what would you like to have?" asked Mr. Hollister. "A doll or a tennis racket?"

Ann chose a cute doll with golden curls.

The excitement continued as other balloons were opened. As they reached ninety-two, Joey Brill rushed in, shoving the other children aside. He had a balloon in his hand.

"Open it!" he demanded.

Pete took out the slip of paper. "Another lucky number!" he cried out.

"Ugh," whispered Ricky to Holly. "He *would* get a lucky number."

"Open it!" Joey demanded.

Mr. Hollister was just about to give Joey a tennis racket when another boy came in with a balloon. Mr. Hollister smiled, saying:

"All the lucky numbers are in."

"Oh, just open mine for fun," the boy pleaded.

Pete did this, and Pam glanced at the slip of paper.

"Oh, Pete!" she gasped. "It's another lucky number. How could there be four of them? We made only three!"

CHAPTER 8

A Slippery Ride

EVERYBODY WAS amazed by the fourth lucky number.

"But there were only three," Holly complained.

"That's right," agreed Mr. Hollister. "Something is wrong here."

All the children and their parents could sense that one of the lucky number winners was a fake.

"Let me take a look at the numbers, Dad," said Pam. "I can tell if I wrote them."

First she looked at the slip of paper in the last balloon brought in. It was all right. Then she looked at Ann Hunter's. Hers, too, was one which Pam had written. The first little boy was very excited. He began to cry.

"Mine is real. Honest it is," he whimpered.

Pam looked at his slip. Yes, it was another that she had made out the night before.

All this while Joey Brill was edging toward the door. Pete spied him.

"Not so fast, Joey," he shouted. "Let's read yours again."

Joey might have got away, but the crowd held him back. Gingerly he handed his slip to Pam.

"Dad, this isn't one of mine," she cried, looking intently at the paper. "It isn't my writing." She turned to Joey. "I'll bet you were the one who peeked in our window last night and saw what we were doing."

When Joey heard this, his lower lip began to tremble. He looked at the floor. Although no one said a word, they were sure he had tried this way to get a prize. "You're not playing fair!" Pam cried.

Joey was scared. With his eyes still down, he ran out of the store and dashed toward his home.

"I'm glad he's gone," sighed Holly, and he was soon forgotten.

The grownups who had come with the children began to look at the many attractive items on the counters, and bought a good many. Tinker and Mr. Hollister, and even the children, were kept busy wrapping up toys and hardware.

After the crowd had thinned out Mr. Hollister sat down to talk to Pete and Pam.

"Your idea was wonderful," he praised them. "This is more business than I've had since the store opened. I'm going to give all of you children a special treat as a reward."

"What is it, Dad?" Pam asked.

"I'll tell you at dinner tonight," their father replied. "It'll be a surprise for the whole family."

That evening Mr. Hollister told them they would all go for a picnic supper in the State Park the next day. He would leave his store at four o'clock.

"Swell!" Ricky cried, bouncing in his chair and nearly knocking over his glass of milk.

The children were eager to see the State Park, which lay north of town on the shore of Pine Lake. No automobiles were allowed beyond the entrance to the park. There were many trails and bicycle paths which led to a pine grove, where there were fireplaces and picnic benches.

Mr. Hollister said that just inside the entrance to the park was an amusement center. In it was a merry-go-round, a roller coaster and other exciting rides.

"Can we go on the 'musements?" Sue asked.

"Any you want to," Mr. Hollister said, winking at his wife.

The next afternoon the girls helped their mother prepare a big picnic supper, which they packed in a special basket. Dave Mead, who came to see Pete, heard about the trip.

The girls helped prepare a big picnic supper.

"Say, you weren't planning to take Zip, were you?" he asked. "Dogs aren't allowed in the State Park."

"We'll leave Zip home," Pete replied.

"How about my keeping him at my house until tomorrow morning?" Dave asked. "Then he won't get lonesome."

Since Dave and Zip had become good friends, Pete said, "Sure. Go ahead."

"Well, I have to go cut our lawn now," Dave said. "See you tomorrow. Come on, Zip old boy!"

By the time Mr. Hollister returned from work, his family was ready to leave.

"Tinker will close up at six o'clock," he told them, as they set off in the car.

When they arrived at the park, the children ran up eagerly to the entrance.

"What would you like to do first?" their father asked.

"Ride the merry-go-round," Ricky answered.

The others agreed it would be a lot of fun to ride on the wooden animals while the gay music played. Finally the merry-go-round came to a stop. Mr. Hollister bought tickets, and the children hopped on.

Ricky grabbed hold of a golden horse and was in the saddle in a jiffy. Holly, who was wearing her dungarees, climbed onto the back of a giraffe. Pete sat on the shoulders of a dancing bear, while Pam, holding little Sue in her lap, rode in a yellow chariot.

"Are you going to ride with us?" Holly asked her mother and father.

Ricky was in the saddle in a jiffy.

"Indeed we are," Mrs. Hollister replied.

She and her husband picked horses which were located side by side. Mrs. Hollister rode sidesaddle, while her husband flung himself up onto his steed as if he were a Texas Ranger, making the children laugh.

Slowly the carousel began to turn. The little whistles tooted, and the drums played. Up and down went the horses. The bear jogged from side to side, and the chariot swayed gently as if it were on Pine Lake.

What fun it was! The children's shouts could be heard above the music. When the merry-go-round stopped, Mr. Hollister jumped off and bought seven more tickets.

As the carousel started for the next ride, Ricky had an idea. He was growing a little tired of just bobbing up and down on his horse. He would shinny up the pole to the roof of the merry-go-round and look down.

Standing on the horse's head, Ricky grabbed the pole and began to climb upward. Suddenly the man in charge of the merry-go-round spied him halfway up.

"Get down from there!" he shouted. "Get down from there before you fall!"

But the calliope was playing so loudly that Ricky did not hear the warning. He climbed to the top of the pole and reached out to grab the bar to which it was attached.

Now the bar was covered with slippery grease, but Ricky did not know this. He reached up.

By this time Mr. Hollister had leaped from his horse and was standing below Ricky. As the boy grasped the greased bar, his hands slipped from it. He plunged downward—right into his father's arms!

Meanwhile, the merry-go-round man had pulled a switch which stopped the carousel. He rushed over to them.

"Whew!" he exclaimed. "That was a close one. Nobody ever tried to climb to the top of the merry-go-round before. Is this your little boy?"

Mr. Hollister said yes, and he was very sorry for the trouble he had caused. His wife was very much relieved that Ricky had landed all in one piece and gave him an affectionate squeeze. But she said:

"Never do that again!"

"I won't, Mother," he promised, "cross my heart."

The merry-go-round man said he had a little boy Ricky's age and knew that they were up to all kinds of tricks. He went to get a cloth for Ricky to wipe his hands on.

"I guess we've had enough riding for a while," Mrs. Hollister said.

After Ricky had cleaned his hands, they walked off to see the other amusements. Pete and Pam raced ahead, but soon Pete was running back to the others.

"They have a brand new ride," he said. "Midget auto racers. Come on and look."

Not far away was a midget race track. On it were six little automobiles.

"They have real motors," Pete said. "May I ride one, Dad?"

Soon Pam was out in front.

Mr. Hollister spoke to the man in charge. The midget autos were very safe, he said, and anybody over ten years old could ride them. Ricky was disappointed when he saw his father buy tickets for only Pete and Pam. But he would play some other game, Mrs. Hollister promised.

As Pete and Pam got into their little automobiles, four other children bought tickets and climbed in. The six cars were lined up. At the word "Go!" they started off around the track.

"This is going to be a real race," Holly said, as she watched.

First a boy with a red sweater was ahead; then Pete took the lead. But Pam kept her car near the rail and soon she was out in front.

The little cars had just enough gasoline to go six laps around the track. The boy in the red sweater began to gain on Pam. One by one the others dropped behind. Pete's car developed engine trouble and stopped on the fourth lap.

"Come on, Pam! Come on!" her family yelled. "Win the race, Pam!"

She could not hear this because the wind was making a rushing noise in her ears. Pam held steadily to her course and crossed the finish line first. A great cheer went up from all the onlookers!

The children's next stop was at the Rocket to the Moon booth. It was Ricky's turn now. On the counter lay six tubes loaded with rockets the size of clothespins. In the rear of the booth hung a lighted moon.

Ricky's first and second rockets went above it.

"Just like the cow that jumped over the moon," Sue laughed.

Ricky took careful aim. *Whiz!* The next rocket went straight through the moon, and he received a prize!

"Hurray!" cried Holly.

"Good for you!" Mr. Hollister said, "and now let's eat."

Mrs. Hollister had a suggestion. "Let's rent bicycles and ride to the picnic spot."

Mr. Hollister thought this would be a good idea. First they walked back to the car to get their picnic basket.

The bicycles were nearby, lined up in racks at the entrance to the park. Pam and Holly picked out the ones they wanted right away and so did their mother.

Ricky selected a small bicycle, and Mr. Hollister, a big one with a wire basket fastened to the handle bar. He put Sue into it.

Pete kept looking about for a bicycle suitable for himself. Suddenly he exclaimed:

"Here's a bike just like the one I lost!"

"Say, that does look like it," said Holly. "It has a scratch on the fender the same as yours did."

Pete knew a way to find out for sure. Only last month, he had put a message in a secret hiding place on the bike. He had written it on a paper and wrapped the paper around the battery inside the bike's headlight.

While the bicycle-renting man looked on in surprise, Pete unscrewed the lens of the headlight. He

Pete knew a way to find out for sure.

reached in and drew out the battery. There was a paper wrapped around it.

Pete opened the paper. On it was printed in ink: "This bike is the property of Peter Hollister."

CHAPTER 9
The Woods' Surprise

"ARE YOU Peter Hollister?" asked the bicycle man in amazement.

"Yes!" the children chorused.

And when Mr. Hollister said that indeed Pete was the owner of the bike, the man scratched his head and exclaimed:

"No wonder I got such a bargain."

"What do you mean?" Mr. Hollister asked.

"I bought this bike a couple of days ago," the man said. "A rough-looking fellow rode it here. He seemed to be in a terrible hurry and offered to sell me the bike for three dollars."

"What did he look like?" Pete asked excitedly.

"Well, he was very tanned and wore rough clothes. There was something funny about him. Let's see, what was it?"

"His hat?" Ricky asked excitedly.

"Yes, that's it. He had a queer little red hat."

"That's the thief," Pete said.

Then Mr. Hollister and Pete explained to the man how the small moving van had been robbed of all their toys.

"Hm," the bicycle man said thoughtfully. "I'm sorry to hear that. I guess I'll have to give you the bike."

Mr. Hollister said he did not want the man to lose the three dollars he had paid for the bicycle.

"Tell you what I'll do," the man said. "I'll charge you three dollars to rent these bikes, and that'll even things up."

"Fine," Mr. Hollister agreed, "and I'll tell the police about this at once. It may help them catch the thief."

Pete was mighty glad to have his bicycle back, and hoped he never would lose it again. But just in case he put the note around the bulb once more before screwing it in.

The family set off for the picnic spot. What an exciting ride! They went uphill and down, and when the children coasted down the little knolls ahead of their parents, they shouted and yipped like a bunch of cowboys.

Pete soon had a fire roaring under the grate.

The Hollisters passed several groups of picnickers. All of the fireplaces seemed to be in use. After a ride of about twenty minutes, the Hollisters coasted into a little valley. After rumbling over a tiny bridge, Holly spotted another picnic grove. It was well shaded by tall trees and a little brook gurgled alongside it.

"It's a swell place," Ricky shouted. "I'll bet Indians used to camp here."

Mrs. Hollister agreed that they might have, and suggested that Ricky try looking for Indian arrowheads.

They all got off their bicycles. Pete ran to a pile of wood alongside the stone fireplace. With Pam helping him, he soon had a fire roaring under the grate. Then Mrs. Hollister opened the picnic basket.

"Yikes," Ricky shouted. "Frankfurters!"

He wanted to nibble one right away, but his mother said he must wait until they had been roasted over the fire. In the meantime he could gather twigs.

"May I cook the franks?" Pam asked, reaching for the string of frankfurters.

"All right," Mrs. Hollister said. "I'll get a knife and cut them apart."

She had not gone far, and Pam was looking at the fire when she felt a yank on the string. Turning, she saw a big brown dog with the frankfurters in his mouth! He ran off, dragging the string of them behind him.

"Stop!" Pam cried out, racing toward him. "Drop those!"

The dog gained on her with every leap.

The dog ran into the woods, with Pam going pell mell after him. He scampered through bushes and around tall trees.

Pam lost sight of him twice but came upon the animal again on the bank of a little stream. He was sitting on his haunches devouring one of the frankfurters. When he saw Pam, he started to growl.

"Oh, dear, what'll I do?" Pam thought.

By now the dog had a second one in his mouth. "I must get them back!"

As she went closer to the animal, he growled louder. But Pam bravely reached down and grabbed one end of the string and pulled hard. The angry dog pulled at the other end. Finally one of the links broke and both the dog and Pam tumbled backward. The dog had only two frankfurters and Pam had ten.

When the animal saw this, he leaped toward the girl. Screaming, Pam raced away from him, but the dog gained on her with every leap.

"He'll bite me," Pam thought wildly. "I must do something quick!" Up ahead she saw a tree with a low branch. She leaped up and swung onto it just as the dog lunged for her.

As fast as she could, Pam climbed to the upper branches, still clinging to the frankfurters. The dog stood under the tree, jumping and barking furiously.

Pam cried out for help, but her family was a long way off. How long would the dog stay under the tree?

Suddenly she heard a voice nearby. "I'll get him, young lady."

Out from the trees stepped a park policeman waving a club. He smiled up at Pam. Then he ran toward the dog, chasing him out of sight.

Pam climbed down. As she reached the ground, her family came running up.

"I saved most of 'em," Pam cried, holding up the frankfurters. "Only four missing."

She told her story and the others gasped.

"You're real brave," Holly said, "but I'm still hungry."

They hurried back to the picnic spot and the boys roasted the frankfurters after washing them.

When they had finished eating, the children gathered up the scraps and put them into a big container.

"Let's play games," Pete suggested.

Holly said she would like to play giant steps, so the children did this.

"I'm going to hunt for arrowheads," Ricky said after a while. He disappeared into the thick pine trees, but in a few minutes came rushing back. He was holding his finger to his lips.

"Sh!" he whispered. "Don't make any noise. I found something wonderful."

"What?"

The little boy did not reply. He merely motioned the others to follow him.

On tiptoes they walked behind Ricky. Soon they came to a clearing in the woods. In the middle of it stood a baby deer.

"Oh, isn't it cute!" Holly whispered.

The mother deer nuzzled the fawn gently.

Just then there was a rustling in the bushes. A big mother deer stepped out into the clearing and walked toward her baby. She nuzzled the fawn gently.

"She's kissing her baby," Sue said.

With that the deer looked up and saw the Hollisters. But she did not run.

"They must be tame ones," Pam observed, as the deer gazed at them with their lovely brown eyes.

"Sure they are. I was patting them," confessed Ricky.

Slowly the children walked toward the deer and finally patted them.

"Can you ride a deer?" Ricky asked, thinking how nice it would be to bound around on one of the pretty animals.

"I don't think so," Mr. Hollister said. "Although far away in Lapland, little Lapp children sometimes ride on reindeer."

Ricky decided to try this. He leaped on the mother deer's back, but instead of getting a ride, he was tossed off. Both deer dashed away into the woods.

After Ricky picked himself up, the Hollisters returned to the picnic grove and took another ride before pedaling back to the park entrance.

"Did you have fun?" the bicycle man asked, as he put the bikes into the racks.

"Super!" Pam said, and told of their adventures.

The empty picnic basket and Pete's bike were put into the back of the station wagon. Then the Hollisters set off toward Shoreham.

"A searchlight's shining on our house!"

By the time they came to their street, it was growing dark. Sue had fallen asleep in her mother's arms and everyone was tired.

As they neared their house, the Hollisters were startled at what they saw. Pete cried out:

"A searchlight's shining on our house!"

"There's a police car!" Mr. Hollister exclaimed.

"Goodness," Mrs. Hollister said. "What has happened?"

When the station wagon stopped in the driveway, the children's father hopped out and ran toward the car. A young policeman was sitting in it.

"What's going on, officer?" Mr. Hollister asked.

The policeman stepped from the car and introduced himself, saying he was Cal Newberry of the Shoreham force.

"We got a call that there was a prowler around your house, Mr. Hollister," he said. "The sergeant and I came out to investigate. He's around back looking now."

Just then from the rear yard came the police sergeant, accompanied by Mr. Hunter, the father of Jeff and Ann.

Mr. Hunter explained that he had seen a man walking around the house just as it was growing dark, and called the police. But the sergeant could find nobody.

"Too bad Zip wasn't here to guard the house," Pete said.

"I think we'd better look around once more," the sergeant said.

The Hollisters and Officer Cal joined in the search. They looked under the bushes and behind the trees, then tried the doors of the house.

Suddenly Pete shouted. "Look, Dad, the cellar window is open a little."

This window was concealed by a low bush, and the sergeant had not noticed it.

"Maybe Joey broke in to get the cats," Pam said.

Quickly Mr. Hollister unlocked the front door. The children raced to the cellar. There in the corner lay White Nose and the kittens.

"Oh, I'm so glad," Holly said happily.

Meanwhile Officer Cal was examining the ground outside the cellar window. He called in.

"There are some footprints here," he said.

"Small ones?" Pete asked.

"No, they are a man's prints."

Mr. Hollister explained about the prowler who had been bothering them since they moved to Shoreham.

"We'll keep an eye on this place," the policeman said. "I'll drive past here a couple of times every night until this mystery is cleared up."

The children hurried upstairs and walked with the policeman to his car. Nice Officer Cal turned off the searchlight, said good-by, and the car started off.

As the children returned to the house, the hall lamp made a path of light. In it Pam spied a piece of cloth lying half hidden beneath a big azalea bush. She picked it up.

"Here's a clue," she cried, hurrying into the living room, where her parents were.

"Why, it's a handkerchief," her mother replied.

"Look, Dad, the cellar window is open!"

Pam held up a large red one for the others to see.

"It's a workman's handkerchief," Pete said. "You know who has one like it?"

"Who?" Ricky asked.

"Roy Tinker. I saw one in his back pocket at the store the other day."

"Roy Tinker?" Mr. Hollister said.

"Jeepers, Dad," Pete remarked. "Do you suppose Tinker is the prowler?"

CHAPTER 10
Zip Plays Horse

COULD TINKER have been the prowler at their house?

"Oh, I hope not," said Holly.

"Maybe you should get in touch with him," Mrs. Hollister suggested to her husband.

He nodded and went to the telephone. He called Tinker and asked him to come over right away. In a few minutes the clerk rang the doorbell, and Mr. Hollister brought him into the living room.

"Tinker, is this yours?" he asked, holding up the handkerchief which Pam had found.

The old man looked up in surprise.

"Yes, sir, it is," he answered.

Mr. Hollister explained that it had been found on their front lawn.

"I guess I dropped it here tonight," he confessed.

"You were here?" Pete blurted.

Tinker explained that he had wanted to see Mr. Hollister about a delivery to be made the next morning. As he was walking toward the Hollister home, he saw somebody run into the back yard.

"I wanted to see who it was," Tinker said, "so I followed him. But when I got there, nobody was in sight."

"Did you hunt any farther?" Mr. Hollister asked.

Tinker shifted from one foot to the other uneasily.

"I heard a police siren far down the street," he said. "I didn't want to be caught prowling around your house, so I hurried away. I was going to tell you about the man in the morning."

"I see," said Mr. Hollister. Then they talked about the delivery.

"Before you go," Mr. Hollister added, "please show me where the prowler was."

They went outside, and Tinker pointed out the spot where he had last seen the man. It was exactly the spot where the shrubbery concealed the cellar window!

"That man did climb in!" Pete cried.

"I think we should search the cellar again," Mr. Hollister said. "Maybe we missed a clue."

They all went down and began looking around. Even little Sue was wide awake now, and imitated her brothers and sisters as they hunted for a clue. Suddenly she leaned down and picked something from the fireplace.

"Look what I found, Pammie!" she said, and opened her hand to show her sister.

In it lay a pretty stone. It was white with pink stripes.

Pam gasped. "It's just like the ones on Blackberry Island. Remember, the ones that looked like little Easter eggs? Holly, did you put any of your pretty stones in the fireplace?"

Holly said indeed not. They were in her dresser drawer. Why?

"Look what I found, Pammie!"

Pam quickly showed the clue to the others, and explained that there were many of these stones on the shore of Blackberry Island.

"Dad," she asked, "do you suppose that somebody who lives there has been prowling around our house?"

Mr. Hollister did not think this likely, because no one lived on the island. Tinker was sure, too.

"But this has gone far enough," Mr. Hollister said with determination. "We're going to catch this intruder."

"How?" Pam asked.

Their father gave them a mysterious look. "I'll tell you all about it when I come home from work tomorrow," he said. "But I'll give you a little hint. We'll take his picture!" This was all he would tell.

After the children had had a snack of milk, bread, peanut butter and jelly, they went to bed. Mr. Hollister made certain that the house was locked tightly, although he doubted very much that the prowler would return again that night.

The next morning the children were awakened by the barking of Zip. Pete looked out of his window to see Dave racing around the yard with the dog.

"Hi!" Pete called down.

"Come on out, you sleepy heads. I have a great idea I want to tell you about."

It was true that the Hollister children had slept later than usual. They had raced around so much at the State Park the day before that each of them needed a good long rest.

Once aroused, however, they quickly dressed and hurried downstairs to breakfast. After they had eaten, they all went into the yard to find out what Dave's new idea was.

When Pete asked him, Dave said, "A dog cart. Zip could pull it."

The boy explained that he had seen pictures in a book showing children in Belgium riding in a cart pulled by a dog.

"Gee, that sounds swell!" Pete exclaimed.

"I could drive it all over town," Holly said, "and give Sue a ride in it, too."

All the children were enthusiastic about Dave Mead's idea.

"We girls can make the harness," Pam suggested, "while you boys make the cart."

"Let's do it right away," Dave decided. "I'll go home and get a picture of the Belgian dog cart. And we can make ours just like that one."

He raced from the yard and in a few minutes was back with the picture book showing the dog cart. Pam got a paper and pencil and made a sketch of how the harness was put together.

"We have a couple of old wheels in the garage," Ricky suggested. "We could use them."

Dave added that there was an old baby carriage in his barn.

"I used to ride in it when I was little," he said. "I don't think my mother would mind if we used the body for our dog cart."

Pete, Ricky and Dave hurried off to the Mead barn, while the Hollister girls raced inside the house to talk to their mother. When they told her what they planned to do, Mrs. Hollister said they might use a few old leather belts that she had put away.

As Pam and Holly cut the belts into strips for the harness, little Sue, who was watching, piped up:

"We haven't asked Zip how he would like this. Maybe he won't like to pull a dog cart."

"Gee, that's right," Holly replied. "Suppose Zip is pulling the dog cart and suddenly sees a rabbit. Then what?"

"We'll stop him," said Pam.

In a few hours the boys returned with a cut down body of an old baby carriage. They hurried into the garage with it. After a lot of hammering, the boys pulled a funny-looking contraption onto the lawn. Two coaster wagon wheels were attached to the bottom of the old carriage.

"Now we have to get shafts that will fit on either side of the dog," Pete said.

Ricky knew right away where to find them. He had seen a couple of old clothesline props on the other side of their garage.

Pete sawed the props into the proper lengths, and the three boys attached them to their new cart.

"Let me try it out," Ricky begged excitedly. "Make believe I'm Zip."

The boys attached the shafts to their new cart.

He backed in between the shafts, holding one in each hand. Then he started to gallop around the outside of the garage.

"Hey! Not so fast!" Pete warned as the cart took the corners on one wheel, but his brother paid no attention.

On the next turn the cart fell over on its side! The wheels and shafts broke loose from the body, which then turned over three times and landed upside down.

"Now look what you did!" Dave exclaimed in dismay. "We'll have to build it all over again."

"I'm sorry," Ricky replied, crestfallen. "I'll help." He added with a twinkle, "But it was a dandy wreck, wasn't it?"

"Oh sure," Pete replied good-naturedly. "You ought to be on television."

The boys went to work immediately rebuilding the cart, only this time they made it twice as strong. As they wheeled it toward the house, the girls appeared at the back door.

"We have the harness all ready!" Pam exclaimed. "We've even tried it on Zip for size and it fits."

"We need reins," Holly said, and Mrs. Hollister gave them some clothesline. The children whistled for Zip. The dog came bounding out of the bushes, and licked Pam's hand.

"Will you be a good horse dog and pull our cart for us?" Sue asked as she petted him.

Zip looked at the cart and wagged his tail.

"He means yes," Holly said. "Let's put him in the harness."

Pam led Zip around the yard.

At first Zip did not know what the children were doing and he wriggled around. Pam said, "I think I had better lead him along first so he won't get frightened."

Ricky got into the cart, and Pam led Zip around the yard.

"Oh boy, this is keen! He's really pulling it swell!" he exclaimed.

"I think Zip is trained enough," Pam said. "I'll drive the cart this time." She hopped in. At Pam's gentle guiding, Zip trotted around the yard, just as if he had been pulling a cart all his life!

After each of the older children had taken two rides, Holly and Sue got in. They were halfway around when somebody called from the sidewalk:

"Yah, yah, all you sissies are riding in a baby carriage. It looks funny. Ha ha!"

"Oh, that Joey Brill!" Pam exclaimed, as she saw the boy coming down their drive.

"I want a ride in that!" Joey demanded when he saw what fun they were having.

Pete spoke up. "If you think it's sissy stuff, you just won't get a ride."

At this moment Holly and Sue were in the cart, and Zip was trotting around very proudly.

"Oh, I can't, eh?" Joey said, sneering. "Well, I'll get even with you."

With that, he cried out, "Zip, a cat! A cat! S-s-s-s-t! Get 'im! Get 'im!"

Although Zip was ordinarily calm while playing with children, he stopped abruptly when he heard the word cat and pricked up his ears.

"Up that tree! Up that tree!" Joey shouted again.

Zip whimpered and raced over to the tree Joey was pointing at. The dog raised up on his hind legs and put his paws on the trunk of the tree to get a better look into the branches.

As he did, the children shouted, for the cart tilted up on one end. Holly and Sue tumbled out head over heels onto the grass!

"Now see what you've done!" Pam cried out.

"You'd better get out of here quick!" Pete threatened, racing toward the bully.

Joey decided he would not wait to be involved in a fight because Pete was really angry. He raced off down the street, as the children helped the girls up.

Holly and Sue tumbled out head over heels.

"Are you hurt?" Pam asked.

Sue was crying a little. "We're—we're not hurted, just scared," she said.

But she did not want to ride any more. The others rode the dog cart around the yard during the afternoon. When their father came home, he laughed to see Zip—who by this time was weary—pulling the cart.

Pete suggested that perhaps the dog cart could be used for delivering packages for *The Trading Post*. But Mr. Hollister shook his head and said with a chuckle:

"I'm afraid poor old Zip would really lead a dog's life if we did that. Let him loose and give him some meat and a big bone for his day's work."

As Holly went to do this, Pam asked her father how they were going to take the prowler's picture. "You said you'd let us know," she teased.

Her dad put his arm around her shoulder. "It's easy," he said.

He quickly outlined his plan to the children. Pete had a flashbulb camera that developed pictures right inside of it. They would set it in the cellar so the prowler would take his own picture! "That's great!" said Pete.

After supper he and his father went downstairs to set the trap. Pete picked up his camera which had a string attached to the shutter. His father helped him stretch the string across the cellar window and the outside door.

"If anybody comes in and touches the string, the camera will sure take his picture," Pete said excitedly.

The children could hardly wait for morning. Pete even kept Zip in his bedroom so that he would not scare the prowler away.

Though all was quiet in the house that night, Mr. Hollister did not sleep much. But he heard no sounds to make him get up.

Next morning he and the children hurried downstairs. Pete was the first one to reach the camera.

"Dad!" he exclaimed. "The flashbulb has been set off. We have a picture of the prowler!"

CHAPTER 11
A Mischief Maker

EVERYBODY WAS excited as Pete took the film out of his camera. The children and their father crowded around to see the picture.

When Pete held it up, everybody began to laugh. It was a picture of White Nose!

"Well, I'll be a monkey's uncle!" Mr. Hollister exclaimed, shaking with laughter. "We forgot to take the cat out of the cellar. She pushed against the string, and the camera took her picture."

"Say, it's a good one, too," Pete said, grinning.

"Guess we'll have to try again," Ricky said, sighing. "Let's do it tonight."

"All right," Mr. Hollister agreed.

After breakfast, he asked if the children would do him a favor between one and two o'clock. He had to make a speech before the Shoreham Business Men's Club, which he had joined only a few days before. Since Tinker had to make some deliveries at that time, would the children come down and help?

"Oh yes, Dad," they chorused, even little Sue.

"That's fine. Glad to hear you're all willing to help."

"Dad," Pam said, looking proudly at her father, "it's very nice that the men want you to make a speech."

"They hardly know you, John," Mrs. Hollister remarked, smiling. "It's a great compliment."

Her husband grinned at the praise. He explained that the businessmen wanted him to tell them about his inventions and how he got his ideas for them.

"I guess they just like you, Dad," Pete added. The boy admired his father greatly, and had often told Pam that he wanted to be just like him when he grew up.

"Well, I know another thing I'm going to mention in my talk," Mr. Hollister said, his eyes twinkling.

"What, Daddy?" Holly asked.

"You children. I'm going to tell the men how much you have helped me make *The Trading Post* a success."

"She's strutting just like a girl with a new dress."

He kissed them good-by and left the house. Soon afterward Holly skipped off to her room. She was very quiet for a long while, and her mother wondered if she might be getting into some mischief. She was about to call her when Holly came downstairs with a squirming bundle in her arms.

"Look, Mother," she said. "Something I've been wanting to do—dress White Nose in doll clothes!"

The pet was dressed in a fluffy pink dress, tied at the neck with a little black bow. On her head was cocked a perky blue poke bonnet, and shoes of the same color were tied to her hind paws.

By this time the other children came running to look at White Nose. Holly forgot to hold her tightly, and she jumped to the floor.

"Can she walk with those clothes on?" Ricky asked.

At first White Nose stood still. Then she pulled at the dress with her teeth a couple of times.

"Stop, White Nose!" Holly urged her. "Walk!"

The cat looked at her a moment, then started slowly off, lifting each foot very high to avoid tripping on the dress.

"She's strutting," Pete said with a chuckle, "just like a girl with a new dress."

"Oh, is that so?" Pam retorted. "White Nose probably thinks she's a drum majorette in a parade."

At the word parade, Ricky's eyes lighted up. "Zowie!" he exploded. "Let's have an animal parade. Right now!"

"We could dress all the kittens, too," Pam said.

Jeff arrived with his duck.

"That's 'dorable," Sue piped up. "I'll find 'em." She picked up White Nose, saying, "Come on, kitty, show me where your babies are."

"If we're going to have an animal parade," Pete said, "perhaps our friends would like to enter their pets in it."

"Hey, that's a good idea," Pete shouted. "Dave Mead has a raccoon and Jeff Hunter a duck!"

"Ann has two hamsters," Holly added, "and Donna Martin a turtle."

"That would be swell," Ricky said. "And we can fix up the cart like a fire engine. Zip can pull it just like in a real parade!"

The children scattered in all directions to prepare the animal parade. Half an hour later the Hollister back yard was full of activity.

Jeff had arrived with his duck. Around its neck was a big red ribbon. Dave was leading his raccoon by the collar as the bright-eyed animal rolled over and over on the grass.

Donna was trying to get her turtle to make friends with Ann's hamsters, but the pets were not paying much attention to one another.

Soon Pam and Sue appeared, carrying the five kittens in a basket. Smoky and Midnight were dressed in boy doll clothes, and Tutti-Frutti, Snowball and Cuddly were dressed in doll clothes like their mother.

When the girls set the basket down, the kittens hopped out. How funny they looked as they walked about on the lawn meowing and swishing their tails! Cuddly spied a grasshopper and chased it. The other kittens skittered along behind her as the children shouted in delight.

Presently Ricky appeared at the door of the garage pulling the dog cart. What a change had taken place in it! The sides were covered with red paper. Inside the cart was the green garden hose wound around a piece of log. On the side of the cart hung a step ladder, fastened with two nails.

"That's neat!" Dave shouted. "It looks like a real fire engine."

"Now we can start the parade," Pam called out. "Here, Zip. Let me harness you."

The collie obediently trotted up to Pam, who fastened the leather straps around him.

"Zip can lead the parade," Ricky suggested.

But Holly and Pam reminded their brother that in real parades the fire engines came near the end.

"I think Dave's raccoon should lead it," Pete said.

After a few moments' discussion, it was decided that the raccoon should be first. White Nose would come next with her kittens, then the duck, the hamsters and the turtle. Ricky would bring up the rear with the fire engine.

As the children tried to get their pets to line up, Donna and Jeff suddenly realized that the hamsters and the turtle might not be able to keep up with the others.

"Then we ought to put them on a float," Sue said.

"Good! Let's do it," Ann agreed. "What will they ride on?"

"My coaster wagon," Jeff said.

The others thought this would be fine, and Jeff ran down the street to his house. In a few minutes he returned with his shiny blue wagon, and the pets were lifted into it.

"Now we're all ready to march," Pete said. "Gee, I wish we had some music."

The raccoon started off nicely, with the duck waddling behind.

Mrs. Hollister, who had been happily watching the children from the porch, called out to them, "If you'll wait a moment, I'll bring out the small phonograph."

"Let's play *The March of the Jolly Puppets*," Pam cried excitedly.

Mrs. Hollister quickly set the phonograph on the grass and put on the favorite record. As soon as it began to play, Pete called:

"Forward march!"

The raccoon started off nicely, with the duck waddling behind. White Nose, her head high, led the procession of kittens. Ann pulled the wagon with the hamsters and the turtle, and Zip walked along with the fire engine, as Ricky proudly held the reins.

"They seem to know they're marching to music," Pam laughed as the animals circled the yard.

"My duck never behaved so well before," Jeff said. "He's a real marching duck!"

After the first time around, the raccoon came closer to the phonograph. He stopped to look at the turning record for a moment, but Dave gave him a little push, and he went on.

As the fire engine passed the phonograph, Zip turned his head to snap at a bug in the grass. Suddenly one wheel of the cart banged the phonograph. The needle slipped, making a loud *eeee-kkkk!*

This frightened the duck who flapped his wings and flew a few feet into the air, landing on the raccoon's back. The raccoon started to run around in circles, and dashed through the line of kittens.

The animals were racing around the yard.

"Hey, stop!" Pete shouted. But his cry only added to the commotion.

In a few seconds all the animals were racing madly around the yard, with each child chasing his own particular pet.

Dave caught his raccoon in the top of a tree. Jeff's duck landed on the garage roof and the boy had to climb up after him. Ann got her hamsters from under the porch.

White Nose and her kittens seemed to be the smartest of all. They had run onto the porch, and from the rail sat watching the others.

"It was such a swell show," Dave remarked as he said good-by, "you should have sold tickets to it."

After their playmates left, the Hollister children sat down to lunch. Then just before one o'clock, Mrs. Hollister drove them all over to *The Trading Post*.

On the way, Pete whispered to Pam, "Dad must think we're good salesmen. I hope we sell a lot while he's gone."

When they arrived at the store, Mr. Hollister told Tinker that the children would keep store. Then he went off to make his speech.

Hardly was he out of the door, when the telephone rang. Mr. Hunter wanted five gallons of paint. Would someone please deliver it immediately?

Tinker asked the children what he should do, and Pete assured him they could take care of the order while he made his deliveries. Pete got an express wagon and took the paint to Mr. Hunter.

Meanwhile the other children had taken their places behind the various counters.

All except Sue. She skipped over to the water cooler and took a paper cup. She liked to hear the water go *gurgle gurgle* in the big glass container when she pushed the button. Sue drank a cupful and then pressed the button for another drink.

"Don't drink all the water, Sue," Pam called out. "There won't be any for the customers."

The container was almost empty. But little Sue said she was very, very thirsty. She took another drink.

At this moment a man came in. He wanted to buy a toy for his son. As the children made suggestions to him, Sue took several more drinks. By the time the customer had decided on a play garage, the water bottle was empty.

"Oh, dear," Pam said, "now we're going to have to put another water bottle in."

She found one standing nearby. When Pete returned he pulled the cork out with a corkscrew. Then he tried to lift the bottle into place, but it was very heavy.

Pam offered to help him. Together they could barely lift the heavy bottle. It was halfway in place when suddenly it slipped.

BANG!

It hit the floor and broke into several pieces. Water began pouring out.

"Yikes!" Ricky cried. "Look what you did! Dad won't like that."

Pam got a mop, and they cleaned up the water while Pete picked up the pieces of the broken bottle.

"Looks as if we've been more trouble than we're worth," Pete said ruefully. "I hope we can make a good sale to pay for this damage."

No sooner had he said this than into the store walked Joey Brill.

"Tell him to go out," Ricky begged his brother.

Pete said he could not do this. Perhaps Joey wanted to purchase something. Pete walked up to Joey just like a storekeeper, and said:

"What can I do for you today?"

Joey looked mad. "What can you do for me? You can give me my cat."

"I'm sorry," Pete said, "but your cat isn't here."

"Then go home and get her," Joey ordered.

Pete explained that he could not do that now. He had to mind the store for his father while Tinker was away.

Suddenly it slipped.

"You mean there's nobody here but you kids?" Joey said, looking slyly about the store.

"That's right. We're in charge," Pete announced proudly.

Joey said nothing, but walked about the store, touching this and that, as if he were examining articles before buying them. Finally he stood before a table on which were displayed all kinds of tools. He picked up a wrench, and turned it over in his hand.

Pete came up to him. "Do you want to buy that wrench, Joey?"

"No."

"Well then, put it down," Pete said. "You shouldn't handle things that you don't intend to buy."

Joey sneered. "Try and make me!"

As Pete reached for the wrench, Joey put his hand back quickly. The wrench flew from his grip and sailed across the store.

"Oh!" Pam cried, holding her hands up to her face.

The wrench headed for a shelf of dishes. The next instant there was a terrific crash.

CHAPTER 12

Pete's Big Sale

AMID THE cries of the children, broken dishes clattered to the floor. As Pam and Holly hurried to pick up the pieces, Joey Brill rushed from the store.

Pete wanted to chase him and give him a punch on the nose. But Pete felt he should not leave the store again while his father and Tinker were away. He would take care of Joey later.

"Maybe Dad won't ever let us mind his store again," Pam worried.

Even little Sue looked sad. She walked over and sat on the rocking horse but did not rock. If her daddy did not let them come into the store again, she would miss the lovely toys.

Seeing her sister so glum, Holly went over to comfort her. "Don't worry, Susie," she said. "When we go home I'll give you a ride in the dog cart."

Suddenly a woman's voice behind her said, "I'm here to buy a dog harness."

Startled, the girls looked up to see a thin woman wearing glasses.

Sue spoke up. "We have them."

Holly led the way to a showcase in which lay a selection of leather collars and harnesses.

"How large is your dog?" Holly asked.

"Oh, regular collie size," the woman replied.

"Maybe you should have brought your dog along," Holly said. "Then we could measure him."

The woman laughed. "How could I bring Laddie when his harness is broken?"

"We have a collie," Holly said quickly.

"A collie?" the woman repeated. "Maybe a harness that fits your dog would fit mine."

Holly suddenly giggled. "Once we tried our dog's harness on my brother Ricky, and it fit fine. He's right over there. We'll use him for a model. Hey, Rick, come over here, please."

As the woman watched in amusement, the boy hurried over.

"Get down on your hands and knees," Holly said. "We want to try a dog harness for size."

The boy chuckled and dropped to his hands and knees.

"How's this?" Holly said, fastening a brown leather harness over Ricky.

"Why, I'd say it's fine," the woman said, then laughed heartily as Ricky began to jump about and bark.

Arf, arf!

The woman threw up her hands and shook with laughter. "I don't know when I've ever seen anything so funny," she said.

"How's this?" Holly said.

She paid for the harness and went out of the store still chuckling.

"Ricky," said Pam, "you ought to get a dog costume and join a pet show!"

While she was talking, a tall heavy-set man walked into the store. He had broad shoulders and strong arms, which the children could see because he wore a short-sleeved shirt with an open collar.

"Where's the boss?" he boomed.

"Right here," said Pete.

The man looked down at him, and smiled. "You're the boss?"

"Yes," Pete replied. "My father is out, and I'm in charge of the store."

"And are all these your little helpers?" the man asked.

"That's right," Pete replied. "This is my staff."

"Well, I'm very happy to meet you," the man said.

"To tell you the truth, sir, we aren't very happy," Holly said and told the man of their accidents.

"By George," he replied, "I've had an accident, too."

"What kind?" Pete asked.

"I just wrecked my canoe," he said. "I was paddling on the lake and hit an old tree stump under water. It ripped the floor of my canoe right out, and now I'm looking for a new one."

"For a new floor?" Sue asked.

The man laughed. "No, little girl, I'm looking for a new canoe. Do you sell them?"

"Yes, we do," Pete said proudly. "Follow me over here."

He led the way to the back of the sporting goods department. There, lined up in a rack against the wall, were six canoes.

"We have them at all prices," Pete said. "Now, here's this little one—"

"Little one!" the man interrupted. "I need a big canoe."

"Do you have a lot of children to take riding?" Sue asked.

"No," the man said, "I haven't any children, or any wife either. I'm just Bill Barlow, a bachelor. But you see, I'm so heavy, I need a big canoe to carry all my weight."

All this time, Ricky had been watching Mr. Barlow intently. What fine muscles he had! He must be able to paddle a canoe very fast, the little boy thought.

"Here," the man said, "I think this canoe might fit me."

It was the largest of the six canoes, and cost more than the others.

"This is a very expensive one," Pete said, turning over the price tag for the man to see.

"Big man, big canoe, big price," Mr. Barlow said, laughing. "I guess they go together."

"Then you'll buy it?" Pete asked.

This would be a wonderful sale. If Pete could sell this canoe, the profit would pay for a new water cooler bottle and the broken dishes.

"It's a deal," Mr. Barlow said, holding his hand toward Pete.

The boy put his hand into the man's. How strong a grip he had!

"It's a deal," Mr. Barlow said.

"Swell!" Pete grinned. "Do you want us to deliver it?"

The man said yes, and gave his address. As Pete was putting the money from the sale into the cash register, Tinker came back. He spied the broken water bottle immediately.

"What happened?" he asked.

The children told the story of the accident and Tinker brought a spare bottle from the basement and inserted it easily. Mr. Barlow took a drink.

"Quite a lively force of salesmen you have here," he said to Tinker, winking.

"This man just bought the biggest canoe we had, Tinker," Pete said.

"That's right good," the old man remarked, surprised to hear that the children had made such a large sale. "Do you want it delivered right away?" he asked Mr. Barlow.

"Yes, if you can do it."

Tinker said he would be glad to put the canoe on the delivery truck at once. He and Mr. Barlow went to the back of the store and lifted the canoe outside and onto the truck. Tinker got behind the wheel, the big man jumped in, and they went off.

Not long afterward Mr. Hollister returned from the meeting.

"How'd you make out, Dad?" Pete asked.

Mr. Hollister smiled. "Well, I guess the speech was all right," he said. "At least everyone clapped when I finished."

He told them that in his talk he had mentioned the new store, and how proud he was of his children helping him.

"We're afraid you're not going to be too proud of us, Dad, when you see what happened," Pete said.

"Yes, the cooler got all smashed up," Ricky reported. "And Joey broke some dishes."

"That's too bad, but you children couldn't help it."

"Make Joey Brill pay," Holly said indignantly.

Mr. Hollister shook his head. "No, I wouldn't like to do that. We're a new family in Shoreham, and should not make complaints so soon."

They talked it over, and the children agreed with their father that the best thing to do would be to forget about Joey's meanness. When Mr. Hollister opened his cash register drawer, he gave a whistle of surprise.

"Where did all this money come from?" he asked.

Pete explained about the big man buying the canoe.

"Fine!" his father said, slapping Pete on the shoulder. "I think you're a better businessman than I am. That's the biggest sale since I opened *The Trading Post*."

The children were glad that their father was pleased. They had not been a nuisance at *The Trading Post* after all! Mr. Hollister was still full of praise for the children when they arrived home that evening.

"Elaine," he said to his wife, "do you know that Pete made a fine big sale this afternoon? I think we should have ice cream for dessert to celebrate it."

"I've already planned it," she said, smiling.

After supper, the children played outside until it was time to go to bed. Then Pete said to his father:

"Are we going to set the camera up again tonight? That prowler may return."

Mr. Hollister liked the idea, but he said laughingly, "Better put the cats in the kitchen tonight. We don't want any more false alarms."

"That's right," Ricky said with a giggle. "White Nose might want to take pictures of all her kittens."

Pete got his camera, flash bulb and string and went into the cellar. Sue and Ricky followed him to watch. After he had set the camera on a box, Pete carefully attached the string to the shutter. Then he passed the cord across the cellar window and the door, hooking the loose end onto a nail over the workbench.

"Pete is smart, isn't he," Sue said to Ricky. "He's going to take a picture of nobody."

Her brothers laughed. "If Mr. Nobody comes sneaking around tonight," Ricky said, "the flash will go *pop* and we'll get his picture."

"What makes it go *pop*?" Sue asked, stepping closer to the camera. Ricky was eager to show the little girl how it operated. He put his finger near the shutter, and looked at Sue very importantly.

"This little gimmick—" he started to say, when his finger touched the camera. There was a flash of light and a click!

"Hey, look what you've done," exclaimed Pete, who had been busy checking the string. "You've taken a picture, and I think that's my last flash bulb."

"Pete is smart, isn't he," Sue said.

"Gee, I'm sorry," Ricky said, a little frightened.

"It was my fault," Sue said bravely. "But I have a birthday candle you can use instead."

At this both boys chuckled. Pete explained that this would not work and went to look for another bulb. There was one left.

After Pete had reset the camera, the three children carried the cats upstairs into the kitchen, and shortly afterward they all went to bed. There was no disturbance during the night.

The next morning Pete was awakened by Ricky, who could not wait to see what had happened in the cellar.

"Hurry up!" he said. "Maybe there's a picture."

They went down the cellar stairs, and Pete let out a whoop.

"Another picture's been taken!" he shouted, and this brought the others running.

"It couldn't be the cats," said Holly, racing up to Pete.

"We'll soon find out who it was," Pete told her, as he tried the back cellar door. It was locked. The window also was tightly shut.

Whose picture could it be? Was it really a ghost? Pete took it out of the camera.

"My goodness!" Mrs. Hollister exclaimed. "It's a man!"

The picture showed only the back of the man. He wore rough clothes, and on his head was a funny little round hat!

CHAPTER 13

A Strange Meow

"THE MAN with the funny hat!" Pete exclaimed. "He's the one who stole our toys!"

"Then this is more serious than I thought," Mr. Hollister said. He confessed that up to now he had thought the intruder only a harmless prankster. "But he's up to something. And he must have the missing suitcase. I didn't tell you children before, but it contained some important papers that I must get back."

"My goodness! It's a man!"

"Maybe he's trying to find the treasure that's hidden in this house," Pete declared.

"No doubt," his father agreed. "And I believe I'd better tell the police about this."

He telephoned, and, while they were eating breakfast, Officer Cal came. He thought that the clue of the picture was so good that the police should be able to solve the mystery easily.

He suggested that this information be kept a secret. So the Hollisters agreed to say nothing about their latest clue to anybody. Even little Sue promised not to tell her friends.

"But is it all right to tell Annie?" she asked.

"Annie?" Officer Cal asked.

"That's my dolly. She won't tell anybody." The policeman laughed. Then Pam told him the Happy Hollisters thought the intruder was after a treasure that might be hidden in the house.

"In that case," he said, "you'd better find it first."

"We've already looked," said Holly.

"A good detective never gives up," he smiled as he went off.

"Let's play detective," Ricky suggested. "We'll find the treasure and the man with the funny hat and our toys and your suitcase, Dad."

He laughed. "A big order but good luck to you. I'll expect a report tonight."

During the day, the children played detective seriously. When a peddler came to the door, Holly looked up at him and asked:

Holly really had found a treasure.

"Do you have a funny little red hat?"

The peddler looked very much surprised. He said, yes, he had a little red hat which he wore years ago to a costume party, but he had not seen it in years. He supposed it was in his attic.

"Would you like to have it to play with?" the man asked.

Holly said no, that was not the hat she meant. Then the man sold Mrs. Hollister two quarts of strawberries and went away.

That night at the supper table, as Mr. Hollister was pouring cream on his dish of berries, he said, "Well, what did you young police assistants do today?"

"I looked under every bush in our yard," Ricky said. "I thought maybe the treasure was buried somewhere outside. But I did find an Indian arrowhead." He held up the prize in his hand.

Holly reported that she had searched in the garage. She really had found a treasure.

"It was stuck behind one of the beams," she said as the others listened intently.

From her pocket she brought out an old-fashioned coin purse.

"There's a real silver dollar in it," she said proudly.

"That's too heavy to carry around," Ricky spoke up, grinning. "How about using it to buy us ice cream?"

The others laughed, and Holly said she was not going to spend it. She would save it to buy a Christmas present.

Pete told the family he had continued his search in the attic and found an old story book. "But it's for girls," he said in disappointment.

Pam chuckled. "I'll trade it for what I found in the cellar," she said, holding one hand behind her back.

"What is it?"

"Sight unseen," Pam replied, teasing her brother.

"Okay. I'll swap."

Pam held out her hand. It was a tiny harmonica.

"I washed it," she said, handing it to her brother, "and it still plays."

Pete blew a few notes. "This is keen," he said, grinning. "I'll use it to get everybody up in the morning."

"But not too early," his father begged. "I'll be getting to sleep late as I have some reading to do."

He went to bed when the children did but got a book and read for a couple of hours. Finally, he put down the book and raised up to switch off the light. As he did, he glanced out the window.

Mr. Hollister was startled to see a dark shadowy figure cross the lawn and disappear in the direction of the lake front.

"If that's the prowler, I'll get him this time!" he told himself.

Slipping into his robe, he tiptoed downstairs and out of the house. Someone was making a rustling noise on the dock.

As he noticed the person bending over, Mr. Hollister said to himself:

"I wonder what he's up to. Maybe he's going to steal our boat!"

He took a few steps forward noiselessly. Finally he was about ten feet from the dock. In the darkness he could make out that it was a small fellow, just the right size to slip through cellar windows!

"Halt, whoever you are!" Mr. Hollister shouted, at the same time leaping toward the prowler.

As his hands gripped a pair of legs, there was a muffled shout and the person crumpled on the dock.

"Don't move, I have you!" Mr. Hollister said.

"But—but, Dad, it's Pete! Let me up!"

Mr. Hollister released his grip. He stared unbelievingly, then laughed heartily as he helped Pete up.

"I'm sorry, Son. I thought you were our intruder. What on earth are you doing here?"

Mr. Hollister was startled.

"You sure are a good football tackle," Pete said. "I was just setting out some catfish lines."

He said they had already been set, and that he was picking up his can of worms when his father jumped him.

"I don't understand why Zip didn't bark when he heard you leave the house," Mr. Hollister said as they went back together.

Pete chuckled. "I took care of that," he announced. "I put Zip in Pam's room."

Next morning, Pete was the first one out of bed. He jumped into his clothes and ran from the house to the lake front. One of his lines was stretched tightly. Pete pulled it in. On the hook was a catfish two feet long. It thrashed about in the water as Pete lifted it up.

"Hey! Look at this! Look what I've caught!" he shouted.

The other children came running from the house, followed by their parents.

When little Sue saw the catfish, she jumped back in alarm.

"What funny whiskers," she said. "Will it bite, Daddy?"

When Mr. Hollister said it might, Sue skipped a respectable distance away. But she was still full of questions about the fish.

Mr. and Mrs. Hollister walked toward the house, but the children remained behind.

Sue asked Pete, "Why do they call it a catfish, Pete?"

"I guess because it can meow," her brother replied, teasing her.

"You're awful," Pam said. "Sue, it's because it has whiskers like a cat."

"And I think they live among the cattails, too," Ricky put in.

Sue was confused. "Can a catfish really meow like a cat?" she asked.

Her big brother did not know whether to tease the little girl any more or not. He took the hook from the fish's mouth and held the big prize up. Then suddenly a funny look came over his face. The fish seemed to be talking!

"Meow, meow!" it said. This was followed by a purring sound.

Pete's jaw dropped. He looked at Pam in amazement.

"It's—the fish is meowing," he said meekly.

"Sure, that's what you told me," Sue said.

Pam's eyes grew as big as lollipops. Again came the soft *meow meow meow*.

Pete dropped the catfish. This was more than he could stand. A catfish that meowed like a kitten! Even Ricky was a little frightened by the whole thing.

Just then the children heard somebody laugh. They turned to look. Mr. Hollister stepped from behind a tree near where they were standing.

"Do I make a good catfish?" he asked. "You really thought the fish was meowing?"

"Oh, Dad," Pam exclaimed, "you're always playing jokes on us!"

"When you're not playing them on me," Mr. Hollister replied.

"The fish is meowing!" he said.

Pete merely grinned. He ran into the house for a knife with which to skin the catfish. Then he asked permission to build a fire near the dock so he could broil it. Mr. Hollister said this would be all right if the children were careful. He left for *The Trading Post*.

After the fire had been started, Pam brought a skillet from the kitchen with some butter in it. The big fish was cut in pieces and put into the pan.

This was the first time Sue had seen such a thing. She became so excited that she skipped and pranced around the fire.

"Don't get too close, Sue," Pam warned her.

The little girl moved away but a few moments later she was back again. Pete and Holly had gone for more wood. Pam went to get more butter.

Suddenly Ricky who was nearby gasped. As Sue whirled about, her dress touched a sudden flame which shot upward. In a moment it was on fire!

Ricky rushed over to his sister. He pushed her to the ground and began beating out the flames with his hands.

CHAPTER 14
Kittens Adrift

IN A FEW SECONDS Ricky had smothered the flames on his sister's dress. The little girl was crying, but, fortunately, she was not burned. Her brother's hands, however, were scorched.

"Oh, Ricky, look what I've done to you!" Sue said between sobs. "I'm terrible sorry."

The children ran into the house, and Mrs. Hollister praised her son. She put salve on his burned hands, and wrapped a light bandage on them.

"Don't get too close, Sue," Pam warned.

All this while Sue looked on wide-eyed. She promised over and over never to go too near a fire again.

"I'm sure you won't," her mother said.

She asked Holly to play with Sue for the rest of the morning. After they had eaten the fish, Pam helped with the dishes, and Pete trimmed the hedge alongside the garage. When they had finished, Pete decided once again to try to find the prowler whose picture they had taken. He asked Pam to help him.

"I'd love to," she said excitedly. "Where shall we look?"

"We've never searched along the shore," he replied.

Together they started down the pebbly beach of Pine Lake. Many of the people whose property bordered on the lake front were in their yards. Some were mowing lawns, others were repairing their boats. The children asked each one if he had ever seen a man with a funny little red hat.

"No, I never have," they all answered.

After Pete and Pam had walked about a mile, they came to a beautiful garden. An elderly woman was weeding a bed of flowers. When the children approached her, she looked up and smiled.

"Hello, children," she said. "Oh, aren't you two of the Happy Hollisters?"

Pete and Pam looked surprised. They had never seen the old lady before.

"Yes, we are," Pete said. "How did you know us?"

"Oh, everybody in town was interested to know who had moved into the old house," she answered.

"We were told it's haunted," Pam said. "Is it?"

"So they say," the woman replied. Then she asked, "Is there something I can do for you?"

They told her that they were looking for a man who wore a funny little red hat. The woman put down her trowel and held her lips very tight, as if she were thinking hard.

"A funny little red hat?" she said. "Yes, I know someone who has a red hat that I would call funny and little."

The children were so excited that they both began asking questions at the same time.

"Who is he? Where does he live? Can we find him now?"

The old lady smiled at their impatience. "You children will not have far to go," she said. "The man who owns the hat lives right next door."

Pete and Pam were amazed and a little bit frightened. How would they capture the man? Would they get him to admit that he was the prowler? What had he done with their toys, and with the important suitcase which belonged to their father?

"Thank you very much," said Pete. "We'll go now to see this man."

"I hope you find him home," the woman replied.

The next house was only a stone's throw away. As the children approached it, Pam asked:

"How can we ever capture him, Pete?"

"I—I guess we'll just have to grab him," her brother replied.

"The man who owns the hat lives next door."

By this time they were near the steps of the house. Suddenly the front door swung open. A very stout, jolly looking man with rosy cheeks and a bald head came toward them.

"Hello, children," he said. "Are you looking for chores to do? Would you like to cut my lawn?"

"No, sir," Pete said. "We're looking for the man with the funny little red hat."

The man seemed quite surprised. First he looked at Pam, then at Pete.

"I guess you came to the right person," he said. "I am the man with the funny little red hat."

"You?" the children exclaimed together.

They knew at once that they had the wrong person. Such a fat man could never squeeze through their cellar window. And besides, this man looked so honest, he could not possibly be a thief!

"I guess we have the wrong hat, I mean man," Pete stammered.

He quickly told the man about the prowler and the clue of the little red hat. Pete asked him please to keep this a secret, because they did not want word to get around that would warn the thief they were on his trail.

"I'm sorry to hear about your trouble," the man said. "But, you know, there must be many of these little red hats around."

He explained that a farmer friend of his who lived down the road had given the little red hats to his helpers when they worked in the fields. The man had a few left over and had given them to several of his friends.

"That's how I got mine," the fat man said.

"Pete, let's ask the farmer about all the people who got hats," Pam suggested.

The man told them where Mr. Hill lived, and they set off. When they reached the white farmhouse, a kind-looking woman, who was sitting on the porch, spoke to them.

"Are you looking for somebody here?"

When Pete told her they would like to speak to Mr. Hill, she said she was his wife and led them into the big kitchen. Her husband, a strong-looking sun-tanned man, was seated at a table drinking a glass of milk.

"Good morning, children," he greeted them. "Will you join me in some nice fresh warm milk? Just got it from Bossy a little while ago."

Before Pete and Pam could say yes or no, Mr. Hill had poured them two tall glasses of creamy milk. They thanked him and began to drink. They were not used to warm milk but this tasted delicious. Pam told the farmer of their search for a man wearing a funny little red hat, and why. They had heard he had given out some hats.

"Um-m-m," said the farmer, "that is a strange story. Did the hat look like this one?"

He stepped into the hall and brought back a small red hat. Its shape was just like the outline of the one snapped by the flash of Pete's camera.

"That's it, all right!" the boy exclaimed.

"I picked these little hats up at a carnival last year," Mr. Hill said, "and handed them out to my helpers.

"Did the hat look like this one?"

What did this fellow look like—the one who was prowling around your house?"

Pete said that they did not know but he was roughly dressed. This did not help much to identify him, as all the farm hands dressed that way.

"Do they live around here?" Pete asked.

The farmer said no, that most of them were migrants; that is, they came from faraway places and worked at farms wherever the crops were ready to be picked.

"But wait a minute," Mr. Hill said, stroking his chin. "There was one man who stayed around here. He was real thin and had close-set eyes and black hair that stuck up straight. Funny looking fellow. I saw him in town only a month ago, but I didn't stop to talk to him."

"Who was he?" Pete asked eagerly.

"His name is Bo Stenkle," the farmer replied.

"Where does he live?"

"I don't know, but I'll keep my eyes open," Mr. Hill promised.

"We'll look for him, too," Pam said.

The children thanked the farmer for his information and hurried home as fast as they could. When Pete and Pam reached their own yard, and before they could tell the others of the new clue, they saw Sue and Holly weeping.

"What's the matter?" Pam asked them.

Little Sue was crying too hard to speak, but Holly said that White Nose and her kittens were gone. Somebody must have taken them.

"Oh, the poor pussies!" Sue wailed.

"Probably Joey," Pam said.

Mrs. Hollister came out of the house. She said she had seen a boy running across the lawn, but had thought nothing of it until the children noticed the kittens were gone.

"Which way did he go, Mother?" Pete asked.

Mrs. Hollister pointed toward Sunfish Cove. This was a little inlet of shallow water which got its name from the sunfish living there.

"Let's look there," Pete said.

The four hurried toward the cove. What a strange sight greeted them! Far out from the shore, on a wooden raft, sat White Nose and her five kittens.

"Oh, the poor pussies!" Sue wailed. "They'll get drownded!"

White Nose was doing her best to get off the float, but every time she walked to the edge to look for something else to jump on, it would tilt dangerously.

"We have to do something right away," Pam said.

Pete thought he would swim out, but just then he spied a canoe slipping around the edge of the cove. A large man was seated in the back. He was paddling with long, strong strokes.

"Pete," Pam said excitedly, "that's Bill Barlow, the bachelor, in the canoe you sold at *The Trading Post*."

"It is!" Pete exclaimed. He shouted at the paddler.

Bill turned his head. When he saw the children waving their arms, he paddled rapidly toward them.

"Hello," he said. "You sure sold me a fine canoe. I've never had one as good as this."

Pete said he was glad Bill was satisfied. He had a favor to ask of him. Would he please save the cat and kittens out on the raft?

The man looked in White Nose's direction. "I'll be glad to," he said. "How in the world did they get out there?"

"We think a cruel boy did it," Pam answered.

With a few deep strokes, Bill reached the side of the raft. Holding it close to the canoe, he lifted the kittens off one by one into the bottom of the canoe. White Nose jumped in by herself.

"They're saved! They're saved!" Sue cried gleefully, jumping up and down.

The man brought them safely ashore. How the children hugged their pets!

"Oh, White Nose, I thought you were never coming back," Holly said.

The mother cat rubbed her head against Holly's ankles as much as to say, "I'm so glad to be back with you again."

The man in the canoe said good-by and paddled off. Soon he disappeared around the bend in the cove. Just then a boy came into sight.

Joey Brill!

"Did you put White Nose and her kittens on the raft?" Pete wanted to know.

"I'm not saying I did or I didn't," Joey replied.

"Well, if you did, you're horrid!" Pam exclaimed. "I'm glad they don't live with you any more!"

The children put the animals on the ground. At once Joey started to pick them up. As he did, they heard

"I thought you were never coming back," Holly said.

a dog barking. Out of the high grass bounded a large black dog.

With a growl he dashed straight for White Nose and her kittens!

CHAPTER 15

A Trip with Tinker

WHITE NOSE arched her back and was ready to meet the attack. But the big dog paid no attention to her. He sprang directly toward the kittens.

"Go away! Stop!" Pete cried.

Just then there was a blur of yellow fur which seemed to fly over the ground toward them.

"It's Zip," Holly exclaimed. "Zip has come to rescue our kittens!"

Before the black dog could harm the kittens, Zip was upon him. Over and over they rolled in the grass, growling and snarling.

"Stop, Zip! Stop fighting!" Pam cried, as she and Pete gathered up White Nose's babies in their arms. "We have them."

The fight did not last long. Zip was too much for the black dog, who put his tail between his legs and streaked off. Zip trotted up to the children and licked their hands. Joey Brill in the meantime had disappeared.

"I still think he was the one who put the cats on the raft," Pam declared.

The children had come to Sunfish Cove by walking along the pebbly shore. Now, as they returned home, they decided to go back by way of the road. It was a little longer, but easier walking than over the rough stones.

Several people stopped the Hollisters to admire the kittens. One nice woman named Mrs. Elkin asked them if they would show the cats to her daughter Joan. Pam said they would be glad to and followed her along the walk which led to her house.

A little girl about Sue's age was playing in a sandbox. Seeing the kittens, she ran up to look at them.

"Aren't they cute! May I keep one?" Joan asked.

Pam explained that the kittens belonged to them, but if White Nose had any more babies the little girl surely could have one.

Mrs. Elkin went into the house and soon returned with a plateful of sugar cookies. The Hollister children each took one and thanked her politely.

"Where did you get this?" Pete asked.

Joan invited them to look at her other toys in the back yard. As they walked around the corner of the house, Pete saw a sprinkler whirling about on the lawn. It was just like a gadget his father had made for the children—a combination lawn sprinkler and kiddie spray. It had been in the small van.

"Where did you get this?" Pete asked Mrs. Elkin excitedly.

"Isn't it nice?" she said. "Joan has so much fun with it. We can sprinkle the lawn and sprinkle her too."

The woman told Pete that she had purchased the sprinkler several days before from a man who brought it to her door.

"I don't like to say this," Pete told her, "but I think this belongs to us."

"Really?" Mrs. Elkin asked. "I don't see how that could be."

Pete told her of the theft and how they were trying to find the strange man with the little red hat. His name might be Bo Stenkle.

"The man who sold me this sprinkler didn't have a red hat," the woman said, "and he didn't give his name."

Pete looked disappointed. But he asked how the man had brought the sprinkler. It was too heavy to be carried far.

"He brought it in a boat," Mrs. Elkin said. "I saw him rowing across the lake. He stopped right in front of our place and carried the sprinkler up to the house."

This suddenly gave Pete an idea. The man had come by boat. Did he own it? Did he live nearby?

Pete said he would tell his father about the sprinkler. He could look at it and see if it was his.

"That's fair enough," Mrs. Elkin said, "and I hope you find the man with the red hat."

When the children arrived home, they found their father already eating his lunch. They told him about the new clue they had found.

"Good work," he praised them. "So the intruder's name may be Bo Stenkle," he said. "I'll see if I can find out anything about him."

Immediately after he and Pete finished eating, they drove the station wagon to the Elkin home. The woman and her husband were very cordial. Mr. Hollister examined the sprinkler and identified it as his, saying he had made it himself.

"This teaches me a lesson about buying from strangers," Mrs. Elkin said. "I paid that man a good price for it."

"We'll have to stand the loss," her husband said.

Mr. Hollister said they might keep it. Since their little girl liked it, he believed he would make more of the sprinklers to sell at *The Trading Post*.

"I'm very grateful to you," Mrs. Elkin said. She smiled. "I'll stop at your store very soon to buy some hardware and toys."

On the way home, Pete said he had an idea. Would his father allow Tinker to accompany him and Pam to Blackberry Island? If the thief had rowed across the lake, it was possible he was staying on the island.

"Remember the picture of our house Pam found there?" he reminded his father. "And the warm embers in the fire?"

"That's right."

At first his father did not want to give permission, thinking it might be a dangerous adventure, but when Pete assured him that they would be very careful, Mr. Hollister gave his consent.

He drove immediately to *The Trading Post*. It had been a quiet day, so he could spare Tinker. The old man grinned broadly at the prospect of catching the intruder and went to the Hollister home with Pete to pick up Pam. She was thrilled about the adventure, since she liked playing detective as well as her brother.

"I hope we catch the thief today," Pam said as they went to bail some water from the bottom of their rowboat.

Pam offered to do this while Pete and Tinker walked to the garage to get the outboard motor.

"We'd better fill the tank," Pete said, as he helped to lift the motor from a special rack he had built for it.

The boy poured gasoline and oil into a gallon jug and mixed them thoroughly. He carried the fuel to the boat, then went back to help Tinker carry the motor.

By the time they had fastened it in place, Pam had the bottom of the boat thoroughly dry. Pete unscrewed the gas cap and poured in the fuel.

"I think we're all set now," he said, wiping his hands on a cloth.

"We'd better fill the tank."

Mrs. Hollister, who had been watching them from the house, walked onto the dock as Pete, Pam and Tinker prepared to shove off.

"Good luck this time," she said. "Be careful not to separate in your search. That prowler might be a very bad man."

"Yes, Mother," the children said, and Tinker assured her he would take care of them.

When the three had taken their places in the boat, Mrs. Hollister shoved it away from the dock. Pete started the motor and away they *putt-putted* across the lake.

When they were about halfway to the island, Pete looked back toward his own dock. He could faintly see his mother waving a white handkerchief.

Suddenly he spied something else. Another motorboat seemed to be following them. Pete turned his course to the left. The other boat did likewise. Then the boy steered to the right. The boat still kept after them.

"I wonder if that fellow in the boat is trying to play games," Pete remarked.

"Who is he?" his sister said.

"Can you make him out, Tinker?" Pete asked.

Tinker looked hard but said all he could see was a man bending over in the boat.

"I think he's doing that so we can't see his face," Pete said, becoming suspicious.

The boy wondered what to do. He had read airplane stories which told about one plane being pursued by another. It was smart to turn the tables and chase the pursuer.

"That's just what I'll do," Pete told himself.

Warning Tinker and Pam to hold on tight, he swerved the boat about and headed for the man who was following him.

The other fellow was quick, too. He changed his course and headed toward the northern tip of Blackberry Island.

"I can't catch him," Pete said, as he fell behind. "We have too much weight in this boat."

By the time the Hollister boat neared the shore, the other craft was out of sight around a bend in the shoreline.

Pete was careful to avoid any rocks at this time. He carefully steered the boat to the shore. They all hopped out.

Pete swerved the boat and headed for the man.

"I don't know where to begin searching this island," Tinker said. "It's a big one and has a lot of trees and bushes."

"I think we had better search the shoreline first," Pete said. "But let's stay close together."

Before they started, however, Pete had Tinker help him pull the boat far up on the beach. Then the three of them started walking along the shore. After a few minutes Pete cried out:

"I see footprints."

Tinker and Pam ran to his side. There was a circle of prints evidently made by a man.

"Where do they lead to?" Tinker asked.

"Over there," Pete answered.

The children followed the footprints. They ended at an old log lying back from the shore. Pam walked around the log and suddenly gave a little cry.

"My doll! My French doll!" she exclaimed.

The excited girl reached down and picked up the pretty doll with its satin and lace dress, one of her collection of foreign dolls. She had left it in her desk, which had been placed in the little van.

"How did it get here, Pete?" she said, then looked around nervously. "Unless Bo Stenkle is here!"

"I think he must live on this island," Pete answered. "Come on, let's find him."

"That may not be so easy to do," said Tinker. "There are many good hiding places here."

"Can you see any more footprints?" Pam asked.

Tinker and Pete bent down. The boy could see nothing, but after the old man looked intently around at the ground a few seconds he said:

"Yes, I can see that somebody walked from here into the bushes."

The three pushed their way into the dense shrubbery. Soon the footprints disappeared entirely.

"The fellow couldn't have vanished into thin air," Tinker remarked, puzzled.

Pam bent down to examine the ground around her. Pete and Tinker continued their search, walking farther and farther from the girl.

"Do you see anything, Tinker?" Pete called.

"Nothing at all."

"How about you, Pam?"

There was no answer. Pete looked about for her. She was not in sight.

"Pam! Pam! Where are you?"

In a moment came the reply. "Here I am in these bushes. Come over and see what I found."

Pete followed Pam's shout and found her bent close to the ground.

"Here's a real deep footprint," she said, pointing, "and it matches the others."

There were no more nearby.

"The fellow must have jumped," the boy reasoned.

"You're right," said Tinker, who had hurried up to join them. "Maybe he landed on that log."

Up ahead was part of an old tree trunk lying on the edge of a gully, which was filled with trickling water. They examined the log carefully and found a scuff mark.

"My doll! My French doll!" she exclaimed.

"He probably jumped into this stream," Pam said, "and walked along it. Now we'll never find his footprints."

"He's clever, whoever he is," Tinker said, scratching his head.

He and the children were about to return to the shore, when a bright colored object attracted Pam's attention. Something red was snagged on a blackberry bush. They hurried up to see what it was.

"The little round hat we've been looking for!" Pam exclaimed.

CHAPTER 16

The Chase

PETE AND Pam looked closely at the hat. It was just like the one Farmer Hill had shown them. And it looked exactly the same as the one worn by the prowler whose picture Pete had taken.

"He's here on the island, all right," Pete declared. "Tinker, will you help us search some more?"

Tinker said he would do his best. He suggested they take the hat with them for evidence, so Pete stuffed it in his pocket. Then the three set off again.

"If Bo Stenkle's living here, he must have a shack or something," Pam remarked.

"It probably wouldn't be near the beach where he could be seen," Pete reasoned. "Let's walk toward the center of the island."

The three trudged through the thick underbrush. The grass was high and the tangle of blackberry vines made progress difficult. After a while they came upon a thicket of birch trees.

"What's that in there?" Pete asked, pointing among the trees. "A little house?"

Pam and Tinker looked hard at the spot.

"Yes, there is something in there," Pam said. "Looks like a shack."

Approaching the place as quietly as they could, the three saw a small hut nearly concealed by the trees.

"This is a good hideout," Pete said. "I'll bet it belongs to the thief."

Picking their way up to it cautiously, they saw that it had but one room. A tiny porch, half tumbled down, was at the front of the hut. Pete stepped carefully onto the porch and peered through a broken window.

"Nobody's in here," he said.

Pam opened the door, and the three went inside. An old table and a rickety chair stood in the middle of the room. On the floor alongside the table lay an envelope, which Pete picked up. Excitedly he showed the envelope to the others. Written on the front was a name and address:

Bo Stenkle

General Delivery

Stony Point

"We're on his trail!" the boy exclaimed, joyfully, putting the envelope in his pocket. "This is Bo Stenkle's hideout!"

Pete peered through a broken window.

Hardly had he said this when there was a rustling sound at the back of the shack. Pete dashed through a little door at the rear just in time to see somebody racing off through the bushes.

"There he is! After him!" the boy cried.

Pete raced as fast as he could, pushing bushes and low hanging branches aside. Pam and Tinker brought up the rear. It seemed as if they were gaining on the fugitive, when suddenly Pete tripped over a blackberry vine, and fell flat on his face.

The fall knocked the wind out of him. He lay still for a moment until Pam and Tinker helped him to his feet.

Now the man was far ahead of them. By the time the searchers picked up the trail again, they heard the sputter of a motorboat.

"He's gone!" Pam cried in dismay.

"Not quite!" Pete shouted, racing onto the shore before the others.

The boat was about ten feet out, and Pete made a dash for it, splashing into the water. He threw himself toward the boat and grabbed onto the side as it sped into deeper water.

"Hey! Get off of there!" shouted the man in a rasping voice.

Pete continued to climb in, staring hard at him. He had a small head with black hair that stuck up straight. His eyes were close set, his nose thin and his mouth cruel looking. Bo Stenkle!

"Let go!" he shouted again and reached toward Pete.

"Not until you give yourself up," the boy replied bravely, pulling himself over the side of the boat.

Bo Stenkle snarled and like lightning shoved a bony hand at the boy. It caught Pete on the chest and sent him reeling backward into the water. He disappeared.

When Pam saw this, she screamed.

"Don't worry," Tinker said. "Pete's a good swimmer, isn't he?"

But the boy did not come up immediately, and the boat churned away.

"Oh dear!" Pam said nervously, "maybe that man knocked Pete out!"

Then suddenly she saw his head pop to the surface, and with strong strokes he swam to shore.

"Oh, I thought you were drowning," Pam cried as her brother waded dripping wet onto the shore.

"I swam underwater so Bo wouldn't see me," Pete explained.

"Then it was Bo Stenkle?" Pam exclaimed.

"Sure, was. We'll get him yet!"

The children decided that the best thing to do was return to Shoreham and tell the police about Bo. They hopped into their boat, and Pete gave it all the speed he could. It finally went so fast the prow lifted out of the water a little.

"I'll land at the police dock," Pete said and in a little while he drew alongside it and stopped.

"I guess I'd better get back to the store," Tinker said. "You two can handle this alone." He grinned. "You're real good detectives."

He went off, and the Hollisters walked into headquarters. Officer Cal Newberry was on duty.

"Hello, children, what can I do for you?" he said, smiling.

Pete and Pam told their story quickly. The island was the hiding place for the toy thief. They thought his name was Bo Stenkle.

"Here's our proof," said Pete, proudly handing over the note and the little red hat.

"This is amazing," Officer Cal said, and wrote everything down. "I'd like to find that thief."

Cal said he was new in the department and would like to solve a big mystery. Maybe this was his chance.

"Besides," he said, "we can't have a character like Bo Stenkle running loose around Shoreham. I'll see if we have any record on him."

Bo shoved a bony hand at the boy.

Cal opened a filing cabinet and looked through a lot of papers. Finally he exclaimed:

"Yes, here's his name and picture."

"That's the man!" the Hollisters cried.

"He was in trouble at Stony Point last year," Cal said. "He stole a farmer's horse and was caught. But he was let off with a light sentence as it was his first offense."

The young policeman closed the filing cabinet and picked up a telephone. As he dialed a number, he said to the children:

"I'm calling our State Police Motorboat Patrol at the lake to keep close watch on Blackberry Island. I can't go myself, because I must stay at headquarters this afternoon."

Cal told the Lake Patrol officer who answered the phone about the Hollisters' mystery. He said two men would go to the island and would report back at once if they found the thief.

"We'd better go home now," Pam said, so she and Pete left.

When it grew dark that evening, the Hollisters looked over toward Blackberry Island. Every once in a while, they could see lights flashing back and forth.

"It's the police," Pete said.

Would they succeed in nabbing Bo Stenkle?

When morning came everyone eagerly awaited news from Cal Newberry. The telephone rang, and Pete quickly answered it.

"This is Officer Cal," the voice said. "I have just received a radio report from our motor launch police."

"What did they say?" Pete asked excitedly.

"They didn't find anybody," Cal told him. "They're on their way back now. Perhaps you would like to speak to them when they land at the police pier."

"Oh yes, we would," Pete said eagerly, and hung up.

Mr. Hollister had not yet left for *The Trading Post*, and Pete asked if his father would drive him to the police pier. Pam and Ricky wanted to go too.

Mr. Hollister said he would take them.

"Sue, Holly and I are going shopping in town," Mrs. Hollister said. "Suppose you take all of us with you."

"Fine."

They tied Zip near the garage and gave him his breakfast. Then they drove off.

It was not long before they reached the pier. Pete, Pam and Ricky got out and waved good-by. The launch was just coming in. Presently the two policemen tied the boat and hopped ashore. The children introduced themselves.

"Oh, you're the Happy Hollister detectives," one of them said. "Well, I'm sorry to say we didn't locate Bo Stenkle."

"But we'll get him sooner or later," remarked the other officer. "He won't escape us for long."

Ricky was intrigued by the police launch. When the men noticed this, they smiled at the children and asked if they would like to look over the boat.

"I want to look under it, too," Ricky exclaimed. "Does the propeller work with a rubber band like the toy boats Daddy sells?"

Officer Cal was very glad to hear from Ricky.

When the policemen looked surprised, Pete said, "He's only joking."

The officers helped them climb down into the boat. What a big steering wheel it had, Ricky thought. And a motor that could make the boat go faster than any other on the lake, they were told.

"Here's our radio," said one of the men. "Would you like to talk to Officer Cal at headquarters?" he asked Ricky.

The boy thought this would be fun and picked it up. Officer Cal said he was very glad to hear from Ricky, and then laughed when the boy said he would like to be a motorboat policeman some day.

When the three children finished looking over all the gadgets on the police launch, they thanked the officers and started for home. When they arrived, they were amazed to see the back door standing wide open.

"Mother must be back," said Pete.

But no one was around.

"I'm sure she closed this when we left," Pam said, worried. "Maybe somebody's in the house!"

The children hurried from room to room, keeping together. They looked in closets and under beds, but found nobody.

"I guess we were wrong," Pete said as they returned to the living room.

Suddenly Pam noticed that everything in the room was covered with a fine dust.

"Where did this come from, I wonder?" she said.

"Maybe the chimney," Pete suggested. He looked into it, half expecting to see someone hiding up the flue. But he was wrong.

"I know," said Ricky. "It came from the cellar. Let's look."

He unlocked the door, and the three of them hurried downstairs.

What a mess the cellar was! Bricks were strewn all about, and the air was filled with mortar dust. Pete began to cough.

"Look! Look!" he exclaimed to the others. "The bottom of the chimney! It has been torn apart!"

"Look! Look! The bottom of the chimney!"

CHAPTER 17

A Telltale Barn

BROKEN BRICKS and cement were scattered over the floor of the Hollister cellar. Among them lay a crowbar. Somebody had entered the house when the family was away and had ripped the chimney apart!

"Bo Stenkle was here!" Pete exclaimed. "While we were looking for him, he was right in our own house."

"He got the treasure, too, I'll bet," Pam said.

"Let's chase him and get it back," Ricky suggested. "We'll put Zip on his trail."

They hurried into the back yard and untied Zip. How they wished they had left him inside the house!

"Zip!" Pete said, unleashing the collie, "get on Bo's trail, boy! Pick up his trail!"

First he led Zip into the cellar and let him sniff about. The dog seemed to know what was wanted of him. Picking up a scent, he bounded outside, keeping his nose close to the ground.

Pete, Pam and Ricky followed Zip as he went across the lawn toward the street. The dog halted on the corner at the bus stop. Looking up at Pete, he barked as if to say this was where the trail ended.

"Bo Stenkle must have escaped on a bus," Pam said. "Now what'll we do?"

Just then another bus came into sight. It stopped at the corner, as the driver thought the Hollisters wanted a ride. Pete asked him when the last bus had stopped there. The man said about fifteen minutes before.

"Where does it go?" Pete said.

"Over to Stony Point," replied the bus driver.

After the children had told him about Bo Stenkle, the man said, "If that other bus driver picked the fellow up, he'll tell you."

With that he drove the bus off. The children would have to wait half an hour. How slowly the time seemed to pass!

The three children sat on the curb. Finally a bus came into sight from the opposite direction. When they stopped it, the driver said yes, a man answering their description and carrying a box in his hands had boarded the bus at that corner more than an hour before.

"Where did you let him off?" Pete asked excitedly.

"On the other side of the lake," the man replied. "Near Stony Point."

When the driver described the place, the children knew immediately that it was near the spot where the little van had been robbed. They quickly thanked the man, then ran to their house to telephone Officer Cal. He became excited when Pete told him about the new clue.

"I'll be right over in the police car," he said, and they went outside to wait for him.

It was not long before they saw Cal's prowl car. The automobile skidded to a halt in the driveway, and the policeman jumped out.

"We're seeing a lot of each other, aren't we?" he laughed. "Now tell me again, where did you say Bo Stenkle got off the bus?"

After Pete described the place, Officer Newberry said, "I'll go there right away. Suppose you come with me."

Eagerly the three Hollisters climbed into the police car. The officer backed out of the drive and was soon humming along the shore road which led around the lake. It did not take long to reach the other side of the lake and find the side road.

"Here's the place," Pete said, pointing. "This is right where the little van was robbed."

Officer Cal stopped the car. He switched on his two-way radio and spoke to a sergeant at the police station, telling where he was and what he was doing.

Pete spied a man's heel mark in the dust.

Then a voice came over the loud-speaker. "If you need any help, Cal, get in touch with us and we'll send another man out there."

"Right, sergeant."

The children and the policeman hopped out of the prowl car. They quickly searched the roadside for footprints. Finally Pete spied a man's heel mark in the dust.

That was all Officer Cal needed. Being skillful at following footprints, he soon picked up others. The trail led through the thick bushes into the woods by the roadside. The officer said Bo Stenkle evidently had run pell mell.

"No doubt he was afraid someone might follow him."

Finally the tracks led to an open field some distance from the lake front.

"I see a barn over there." Ricky pointed. "Do you suppose Bo is in there?"

"You're a good detective," Cal said. "That would be a likely place for a thief to hide."

Carefully the officer and the three children made their way through the tall grass toward the old barn. Upon reaching it, they found that the doors were locked, but a piece of board near the bottom of one had broken off.

"Let me wiggle in and look around," Pete said.

"Not until I know it's safe," Cal replied.

He peered through the opening and flashed his light around.

"There doesn't seem to be anybody in there. Go ahead. But shout a warning if you see anybody inside. I'll break the door down if necessary."

Pete lay down flat and wiggled his head and shoulders through the hole. Then he pulled the rest of his body through.

It was dark and gloomy inside. When the boy's eyes became accustomed to the dim light, he saw something which made him gasp.

In one corner of the barn stood the rest of the stolen toys!

Pete ran to the big double doors and lifted off the wooden bar that locked them. As the others rushed inside, he cried:

"Our toys! Our lost toys! They're in there!"

"How wonderful!" Pam cried, rushing over to open her desk with the collection of foreign dolls in it.

"Our toys! Our lost toys! They're in there!"

Pete picked up roller skates, a sled and a toboggan, happy to find them undamaged. Ricky was only interested in finding his father's missing suitcase. Meanwhile Officer Cal was searching the barn with the slim hope that Bo Stenkle might be hiding in it. Presently he climbed the ladder to the haymow and poked among the bales stored there.

Shortly afterward Pete looked up to see several barn swallows swoop through a hole in the roof. As he watched them, the boy suddenly saw a man climbing out of the hayloft window.

"Hey, there's Bo Stenkle!" Pete shouted. "And he's getting away!" he added as the thief dropped to the grass. At this point the ground was on a higher level than the front of the barn.

Pete, Pam and Ricky raced outside just as the man scrambled to his feet. Ricky grabbed his legs, while Pam and Pete each clung to an arm.

CHAPTER 18

The Treasure

"LET ME GO! *Let me go!*" the man shouted.

He flung his arms about and kicked his feet, but the children hung on.

"You're not going to get away from us, Bo Stenkle!" Pete cried out.

At this the man looked startled. How did these children know his name?

"Let me go!" the man shouted.

By this time Officer Cal came running from the barn and collared the thief.

"That's enough out of you," he said. "Bo Stenkle, you're under arrest."

The man offered no resistance to the policeman, knowing it was hopeless.

Cal thanked the children for capturing him. "You did better than the entire Shoreham Police Department," he praised them.

Then, turning to Bo Stenkle, he added, "As for you, I have a few questions."

Bo was trembling. He did not want to go to jail. He told Officer Cal he would confess everything.

Before he could say any more, they heard shouts from across the field.

"It's Mother," Pam exclaimed. "And Holly and Sue."

With them was another policeman. Mrs. Hollister was happy to see that her three children were safe. She threw her arms around Pam and then hugged the two boys.

"I'm so proud of you!" she exclaimed upon seeing that Bo Stenkle had been captured.

"They're real heroes," Cal agreed. "I hope you weren't frightened by their absence, Mrs. Hollister."

"I was worried," she replied. "When I arrived home, Mrs. Hunter told me she had seen you all leave suddenly in a police car. I couldn't understand what happened, so I phoned headquarters. I called Dad, too. He ought to be here soon."

Holly began to play her piano.

Just as she said this, Mr. Hollister came hurrying toward them. Quickly the children told him the story of the capture of Bo Stenkle.

"He's going to make a confession," Officer Cal said. "Let's hear it, Stenkle."

The prisoner hung his head in shame. He said he had been living on Blackberry Island. While on his way to Stony Point one day, he had spied the small van by the side of the road with no one in it.

Since he needed money, Bo had robbed the van. He had sold some of the toys and the sprinkler, but the rest of the things were in the barn.

"A suitcase, too?" Mr. Hollister asked.

"Yes."

"Show me."

Bo led them into the barn. He had hidden the suitcase in a corner of a horse stall. Mr. Hollister quickly opened it. Everything was still inside!

"Thank goodness," he said.

Meanwhile, Holly and Sue had found their toys. Holly began to play her piano, and Sue was hugging three dolls at once.

"Daddy," Pete said, walking up to his father, "there's something we ought to ask Bo. What about the treasure in our house?"

At first Bo Stenkle would not answer.

"Come on, speak up," Officer Cal urged. "You're in enough trouble now. You had better come clean."

"All right," the prisoner said finally. "I'll tell you everything I know."

The thief related how he had heard the story of the treasure hidden in the Hollisters' home. He had searched the place before the family had moved in, but had found nothing.

Then the day before the Hollisters arrived, he had discovered that certain bricks in the cellar at the bottom of the chimney looked newer than the others. He was sure the treasure was hidden behind them. But before he could pry the bricks loose, the big van had come.

Bo Stenkle had fled toward Stony Point. It was then that he had seen the little van and robbed it while the movers were off taking a swim. Hearing them say the Hollisters would not arrive until later, Bo had gone back looking for the treasure, but again he had not found it.

"But why were you in our attic when we moved in?" Pete asked.

Bo said it was because of Zip. The dog had been such a good watchdog running around outside the house, that the man could not escape. When someone had started down to the cellar, Bo had scooted up the secret stairway about which he knew. When Pete and Pam came up to the attic, Bo had hurried back to the cellar and escaped out the window. By this time Zip was in the house.

"But you kept entering our house, trying to tear out the bricks in the fireplace, didn't you?" Mr. Hollister asked him.

Bo admitted that he had, but something had frightened him off every time. Then when the children had found the clues on Blackberry Island, Bo said he realized he must act quickly.

"I decided to tear apart those bricks the first time I saw that nobody was home."

"Did you find the treasure when you got the bricks loose?" Pam asked.

The man shook his head, but there was a suspicious glint in his eye.

"Are you sure you didn't find it?" the policeman asked sternly.

Pete was watching the man carefully, and noticed that when Bo shook his head again, he cast a quick glance toward the hayloft.

"I don't think he's telling the truth, Officer Cal," Pete said. "I have a hunch he did find the treasure and hid it somewhere in this barn. I'm going to search for it."

When Bo heard this, he tussled in an effort to get away from Officer Cal, but the policeman held him tightly.

"I think Pete's hunch is going to come true," Cal said.

Pete hurried inside and up a rickety old stairway to the loft. He decided to look first among the bales of hay near the window where the man had jumped out.

It was hard work moving the bales and the dusty hay made him sneeze as he searched.

Pete found an old oil lamp and a broken piece of harness.

"Golly," he thought. "If Bo hid the treasure, he certainly found a secret spot for it." But the boy continued to search, reaching his hands way under each heavy bale of hay.

Finally his hands touched something hard. It was a box, which Pete quickly uncovered and carried downstairs. Bo's eyes popped wide open when he saw it.

"I think this is the treasure!"

"I think this is the treasure," Pete said excitedly, handing the box to his father.

With everybody looking on, Mr. Hollister opened it. Inside were bundles of five, ten and twenty-dollar bills.

"That's a fortune!" Officer Cal said in amazement. "No wonder Bo denied finding it. He wanted to come back some time and get it for himself."

"And now it's all ours," Ricky piped up.

"I'm afraid not, son," his father said. "This doesn't belong to us. It is the property of the former owner who hid it."

"The nice old man who doesn't walk in his sleep after all?" said Holly, and the others laughed.

"We shall return the money to him," Mrs. Hollister said. "It will be a nice surprise for him, I'm sure."

Officer Cal smiled. "I can see why people call you the Happy Hollisters. You make other people happy, as well as being happy yourselves.

"And another thing," Cal said, "you children have solved my first big mystery for me. Thank you. Maybe I'll get a promotion."

He said good-by and led Bo Stenkle back across the field where the police cars were parked. The Hollisters followed and climbed into their station wagon.

As they drove home, the children began to sing. Everybody was gay and excited. This had been their first big adventure in Shoreham. They had solved the mystery of their new home.

Little Sue, who had looked on wide-eyed when the treasure had been found, now spoke up.

"It was such fun today," she said. "Can't we do the same thing tomorrow?"

"Swell," Ricky replied. "I'll help you find another adventure!"

CPSIA information can be obtained at www.ICGtesting.com
Printed in the USA
LVOW01s1745080714

393412LV00019B/1058/P